The Well ☆

The Well ☆

Elizabeth Jolley

Viking

Viking
Penguin Books Australia Ltd,
487 Maroondah Highway, P.O. Box 257
Ringwood, Victoria 3134, Australia
Penguin Books Ltd,
Harmondsworth, Middlesex, England
Viking Penguin Inc.,
40 West 23rd Street, New York, New York 10010, U.S.A.
Penguin Books Canada Limited,
2801 John Street, Markham, Ontario, Canada L3R 1B4
Penguin Books (N.Z.) Limited,
182–190 Wairau Road, Auckland 10, New Zealand

First published 1986 by Viking
Published simultaneously in Canada by
Penguin Books Canada Limited
Reprinted 1986

Made and printed in Great Britain by
Hazell Watson & Viney Limited,
Member of the BPCC Group,
Aylesbury, Bucks

CIP

Jolley, Elizabeth, 1923–
The well.

ISBN 0 670 81103 3.

I. Title.

A823'.3

Library of Congress Catalog Card Number 85-41080

For Leonard Jolley

This book is offered as an expression of thanks to the
Literature Board of the Australia Council and to the
Western Australian Institute of Technology. The final draft
of the book was written this year during which time I have
been receiving a Literature Board Fellowship.

To the Western Australian Institute of Technology I am
indebted for the continuing privilege of being with students
and colleagues in the School of English and for the
provision of a room in which to write. I would like, in
particular, to thank Don Watts, Brian Dibble and Don
Grant.

Elizabeth Jolley
December 1985

'What have you brought me Hester? What have you brought me from the shop?'

'I've brought Katherine, Father,' Miss Harper said. 'I've brought Katherine, but she's for me.'

One night Miss Hester Harper and Katherine are
driving home from a celebration, a party at the hotel in
town, to which Miss Harper has been an unwilling guest.
Katherine had wanted very much to go to the party. She is
under the spell of a succession of film stars, the present
one being John Travolta. She tries to walk exactly as he
walks. Having seen every one of his films several times she
is able to imagine herself, when dancing, as his chosen
perpetual partner. Miss Harper, unable to refuse Kathy
anything, has endured a long evening bearing at least two
insults, one of these, because of the Peter Pan collar, laden
with disturbing implication. She also suffered during the
evening's long drawn-out entertainment a renewal of the
realization of her own changed status brought about by
recent events.

When the end finally came Katherine had insisted on
driving. 'You sit back Miss Harper, dear, and take a rest.'
She had covered Miss Harper's bony knees with a cheerful
tartan rug before taking her place behind the wheel. 'If I'm
to get my test next week Miss Harper, dear,' her purring soft
voice soothed, 'I'd better get in some practice hadn't I.'
With nimble fingers she had quickly taken the ignition key.

The two women do not speak much during the long
drive home. At first it is a moonlight night, dry and clear.

1 ☆

The chill air carries the fragrance of the ploughed earth. Liking this but wishing for the sharp scent of rain on the dusty paddocks Hester thinks to herself, not for the first time, that the nights in the wheat are either moonlit or quite black. As soon as she has this thought the moon seems to slide into a bank of ribbed dark cloud. Raising her eyebrows and shrugging her thin shoulders she settles herself more comfortably in the passenger seat.

Sometimes during the day, when making this long drive into town or from town, Hester thinks about walking instead of driving. Life would be changed completely if a person walked all the way. Sometimes, in the car, she feels tempted to get out and start walking. The road between the endless paddocks of wheat would lie before her quite deserted and she would accept a different view of time and journey. When walking like this, on and on, no one in the whole world could know where she was. The occupation of a small fragment of the earth is known only to the one person who is alone on it. She imagines the feeling of being unseen and not known about while standing in one isolated place. She would be small and safe walking and pausing to stand still low down under the immense clear blue sky. Perhaps, she thinks, her fear might disappear. It might dissolve, dissipate itself into the light, gently moving air.

Thoughts of walking do not accompany night driving, such ideas at the outset of a long drive in a remote place are best put out of the mind.

The only tolerable part of the evening, Hester reflects, was Kathy's dancing. The girl's energetic rhythmic movements and the yellow dress, in spite of Rosalie Borden's unexpected attack, were by her perhaps one-sided standards, superb. She smiles to herself remembering the music and the dancing; Katherine forever imagining herself as John Travolta's rightful partner. And then there was the sweetness of Katherine's thoughtfulness, the way in which she put aside her own wishes to come over, knowing

Hester's weakness for sweet things.

'Miss Harper, dear,' she hears still the piping but gentle voice, 'I thought you'd like the sherry trifle . . .'

Almost nodding off Hester gives way to some profound thoughts. 'Life,' she declares inside her head, 'is like a wood heap. People do things to ameliorate and to alleviate. With one little detail after another people move through life. It is like taking wood from the heap, one log at a time to the fire, or in summer, the slow stacking of one log upon another when a wood pile is being moved or rebuilt.' She yawns.

The road between black paddocks edged with the black shadows of the saltbush is flat and straight. Every now and then swirls of white mist come towards them and sometimes, when there is a dip in the road, they are completely enshrouded as if in a light white endlessly winding garment.

'How the night can change,' Hester says. The surrounding countryside, she adds, could seem desolate and frightening for anyone travelling especially if they had no home to go to. Katherine agrees saying that she for one would not want to drive the long road at night alone. 'I'm so glad we're together Miss Harper, dear,' she says.

Pleasantly lulled with thoughts of Katherine's happiness at the dance and with looking forward to her own warm bed and possibly because of the enormous, even when shared, plateful of sherry trifle Miss Harper sleeps. She hardly notices when they turn off the road onto the track. It seems, when she does rouse herself, that Kathy is driving too fast.

'Katherine! Not so fast,' she warns, 'Katherine! I said, not so fast! Watch the track. You're going too fast. Slow down Katherine! For heaven's sake! Do be careful. You'll have us over in the scrub if you're not careful! Kathy! You'll lose your licence before you get it!'

Katherine slows down, 'I guess I'm still excited Miss Harper, dear,' she says. 'I'm real sorry if I scared you.' She is, carefully, as American as possible especially with the word you. She chatters on telling Miss Harper how exciting it is that Joanna will be with them in time for the town fête. 'Joanna,' she reminds Hester, is really looking forward to the visit. It was a rèal shame that she was three years in that place, only remand Miss Harper dear, because of her boyfriend, remember? And I've such a wonderful idea for our jam and pickle stall. Oh Miss Harper, dear, wait till you hear my idea . . . Joanna and I could be . . . Oh it's all so Romantic Miss Harper, dear, it's love interest!' Katherine sighs, 'Just right now I would so love to be getting married. A double wedding would be nice – Joanna and me both being married. Just think a long drive like this . . .' she sighs again. For reply, Hester gives one of her snorts to which nothing more can be said. Joanna's impending visit is just another detail in the wood heap which is life Miss Hester tells herself. She reminds herself, not for the first time that she is wishing that something could recall Joanna to the safe place where she has been and that she, Hester, could manage to live very happily without this forthcoming visit, this apparently simple thing which carries so much complication.

'Oh Miss Harper, dear,' Katherine says after a short silence, 'could I make some baby clothes for the fête, for our stall – you know little dresses, with smocking, and, I know, little bibs trimmed with lace, I know they'd sell.'

'Babies eat their lace,' Hester says grimly. 'Keep your mind on the road please,' she adds as Katherine pressing her foot harder on the accelerator causes the Toyota to leap on the track.

'Katherine!' Hester's voice is tense. 'Katherine we're nearly at the bend. Slow down! I can see the bend. Slow down!'

'Oh wasn't it a lovely party,' Katherine, in her piping voice, sings:

Dinga Donga Bella Yair Yair
Pussa inna wella Yair Yair Yair
Dinga Donga Bella Huh Huh Yair

'Wow! Miss Harper! I sure enjoyed myself.'

'I'm glad of it, Kathy,' Miss Harper says, 'but do for heaven's sake slow down.'

Pussa inna wella
Hoohah putta inna Huh Huh Huh
Yair Yair Yair
Dinga Donga Bella Yair Yair . . .

'Oh don't keep singing that crazy song!' Hester says crossly. 'I can't think how anyone could think a nursery rhyme could be a song for dancing – whatever that ridiculous thing, supposed to be a dance, was.'

'Aw, you liked it, Miss Harper, dear, it was the pussycat freeze. Did you like it Miss Harper? You did, dear, didn't you? Eh? Eh?' Katherine presses her thumb on the horn. 'And what about the break-dance huh? Eh?'

'Stop the car Katherine, I'll drive now.'

'Weee-wopp-here we go! Nearly home, Miss Harper, dear. Nearly at the last bend. Oops – sorry! caught the bushes, hit a rock. Blast! Shit! Oops sorry Miss Harper, dear, hit the rocks again, always get that rock. I don't hack it.' Katherine laughs in a shrill voice. 'I wish Joanna was here already. Wish you was here already Joanna. Joanna JOANNA'.

'Look out! oh look out! There's something on the track,' Hester's voice, shrieking, is hoarse with fear, 'Look out. Oh God! The bend. Brake! Katherine ! Brake! The bend. There's someone there, someone on the track. For God's sake, child brake!'

Hester stops shrieking suddenly as something hits the Toyota with a dull heavy thud. Katherine stops at once, the engine is still running. 'But there's never ever anyone on this track,' she wails, 'there's never ever been anyone along here, not ever . . .'

Miss Hester grabs her stick and, with difficulty, she climbs out. Leaning heavily on the stick she makes her way to the front of the truck.

5 ☆

'Turn off the lights,' she says. 'We don't know if there's anybody on the track.' And then in a trembling low voice she calls softly, 'It's not a roo, Katherine. It's not a roo. Don't come out, it's too horrible. We've caught something on the bar. Stay there where you are.'

Hester moves slowly round to Katherine's side, 'there's only one thing to do,' she says in the same low voice which is like a hoarse breaking whisper. 'Stop crying! Stop making that noise. I want you to listen carefully and do everything I tell you. We've no choice. We've not got much time. Heaven knows there may be someone else around. We can't know. Now come on. Drive slow. Slow as you can and as quiet as you can. We're nearly in the yard. I'll keep here alongside. When you get in the yard turn straight away and get the bar as close as you can to the well. Yes, I said the well. There's nothing wrong with the Toyota, not yet, just get as near to the well as you can. Yes. I said the well . . .

Hester Harper was no longer young when her father, old Harper, died. In spite of a lame leg which caused her to walk awkwardly leaning on a stick, and in spite of her own advancing years, she decided that she would continue to run the property.

Following her father's ways and wearing all the keys on a gold chain round her neck she concentrated on wheat and sheep; the sheep being able to feed extensively on the endless stretches of wheat stubble when there was very little else for them to eat.

The keys on their valuable mooring were not an ornament but were more of a reassurance. She wore them hidden beneath the bodice of her dress and was able to feel them, every minute of the day and night (when she was awake), nestling between her rather flat breasts. She did not wear rings or ornaments of any kind. Only the keys.

Some time before the death of her father Miss Harper had impulsively taken, partly out of pity and partly from fancy, a young girl, an orphan to live at the farm.

She thought she had never seen the girl in the shop before and was about to ask who she was. The fair-haired girl, though quite pretty, was thin and she had a white face with an anxious, almost squinting, expression. It was the sight of the white face in the gloomy back regions of the shop which caused Miss Harper to want to ask her question.

'Exotic dancers!' Indignation burst from Mrs Grossman, the wife of the storekeeper. 'I ask you! Just you take a look at that out there chalked up on the board for all to see,' she snorted. 'Leather and lace counter lunches, I axe you, see-through bar maids, I axe you who wants to see through to that lot's underwear and worse. It's disgusting! Mr Grossman would rather sit hisself up in the back shed with his lunch in a bag nor have it looking at all that lot. I'll give them fashion revue counter lunches! Whatever next! Leather! Lace!' her face took on a purple shade.

'Since Mr Grossman lives so close,' Miss Harper dismissed the pure-minded lunch eater from his upturned oil drum in the shed, 'next to the hotel, in fact, surely,' she said, 'surely he can have his lunch here at home. He doesn't need to go to the hotel.' She paused waiting till Mrs Grossman's surprised eyelids had stopped their rapid blinking and then asked her question.

'Oh Kathy,' Mrs Grossman, turning her mind with force from the proposed entertainment next door, said, 'yes, Kathy, she's a good girl, good as they come but she's to go back to the Home next week. The Orphanage. Mr Grossman hasn't the business, you see, to keep her.' She lowered her voice, 'Orphans eat you out of the house, you see. And, well, we haven't the trade to keep on a girl.'

'Why did you get her in the first place?' Miss Harper, the daughter of the largest surrounding landscape, demanded. It was her way to be brusque, she knew no other way, and, being kind hearted, she was generous to those less well off and she enjoyed, fully, the respect of the community.

'Well Miss Harper it was this way,' Mrs Grossman said as her deft hands folded the tops of packets. 'Kathy!' she called, 'slip up the yard and ask Mr Grossman to get Miss Harper's kero.' She turned back to her customer. 'As I said she's from the Home, the Orphanage and the Whites had her out at their place to help with the children. She's a good girl, Mrs White says so, but as you know Whites have sold up and they're leaving for England so I said I'd take Kathy but now Mr Grossman says no and when he says no he means it. I'm sorry about it but there it is, there's very little work Miss Harper, to be had in these parts. As it is, our young folk have to go to the city . . .' Mrs Grossman rumbled on. Hester Harper waited for her goods to be stowed in the compact little station wagon she drove and then said if this Kathy would get her things she would take her home with the shopping. 'I will inform the Orphanage of my decision,' she said, 'if Kathy suits me and if she agrees to it she can stay.'

Mrs Grossman was suitably deferential. She accompanied Miss Harper into the street.

'Any time, Miss Harper,' she said, 'if as you shouldn't feel like coming in to town. You have only to send in a note with one of the men and Mr Grossman will be only too pleased to oblige. Mr Grossman will bring you anything you need, just you . . .'

'Thank you Mrs Grossman.' Miss Harper tossed her stick letting it leave her hand as if it were a spear into the long back of her station wagon. She drew on her leather gloves, 'but I am quite able to come to town as often as I need,' she said.

'There you are then Kathy, dear,' Mrs Grossman said quickly hiding her own slack blushing throat in capable hands. 'Don't keep Miss Harper waiting. Jump in quick! There, hold your bag on your lap, that's a good girl.'

Before Katherine could make a suitable reply Miss Harper had started her engine and the roar made conversation impossible.

Old Mr Harper and Mr Bird, who was younger than Mr Harper, were sitting together on the west verandah of the house when Hester arrived home.

'What have you brought me then?' her father, holding his whisky towards the setting sun, said as if asking for chocolate biscuits or sweets supposedly hidden in the groceries being unpacked.

'I've brought Katherine, father,' Miss Harper said, indicating with a toss of her head where Katherine should put the sack of sugar she was dragging across the boards. 'But she's for me,' she added.

'Let's have a good look at you Kathy,' Mr Harper said, 'let's see if your legs are good.' He poked his stick under her skirt flipping the material up. 'Give her a pinch,' he said to Mr Bird, 'on the bottom,' he added. Mr Bird, grinning, leaned forward making a pecking movement with his thumb and forefinger but Kathy, who was nimble, jumped aside.

The men laughed. 'How old are you m'dear?' Mr Harper wanted to know.

'I'll be sixteen in July,' Katherine, in a prim voice, replied.

'It's only father's way,' Miss Harper said later, 'never mind him! I hope you will be happy and comfortable,' she said as she showed Katherine the room she could have for herself.

'Oh, Miss Harper I will. Thank you – thank you.' The girl turned from the room to the doorway where Hester Harper leaned sideways on her ugly stick and, skipping across the carpet towards her, she hugged and kissed her. Miss Harper, taken aback for no one had kissed her for more years than she could remember, said, 'When you're ready I'll show you over the house and explain your duties.' She spoke stiffly because the kiss delivered in this calf-like manner had surprised, even shocked her. For some time afterwards she kept putting her hand to her cheek where the feeling of being kissed lingered pleasantly.

During the evening Hester wanted to enjoy her new acquisition. She felt a need to initiate the girl, to show her something of their life. She played the piano thumping the keys rather as that was her way of playing. She sang some Schubert Lieder in an untrained contralto. She loved these songs, they belonged to a happy time when she was a girl. In her head the songs were perfect. The sounds which emerged bore no relation to this perfection but she did not mind this. The perfection somewhere inside her was enough. She was pleased to see that Katherine sat as if transfixed by the music. It did not occur to her to question whether the girl really enjoyed the performance or whether she simply pretended to while old Mr Harper dozed and Mr Bird sat politely by the fire.

Carried away by the success of her little programme Hester embarked on Brahms, the four serious songs, explaining to Katherine with considerable fervour something of their source.

'Some verses in Ecclesiastes,' she said. 'I expect you know them; *For that which befalleth the sons of men befalleth beasts . . .*' she sang, *'even one thing befalleth them; as the one dieth, so dieth the other.'* She turned the page of the music, peering at it and humming while she tried to remember the words. Her fingers fumbled over the piano till she found the right notes. *'Who knoweth the spirit of man that goeth upward, and the spirit of the beast that goeth downward to the earth . . . Unter die Erde . . .'* She began to remember the German, not sure if she had made a mistake, unable to remember if the earth was masculine, feminine or something between the two. She was surprised as she repeated *Unter die Erde* that her voice could reach such low notes and be so charged with emotion. Surprising too was the sudden memory of the pictures she had fitted to the song when she was a child. Unable then to understand completely she had made secret pictures for herself of water flowing far down under the ground; water seeping over smooth rocks and gathering in small underground pools to swell little rivulets moistening the dark soil in which the mysterious roots of the reeds and the trees found their nourishment. The same images came to her now after all the years in particular when she let her voice go down, as it were, under the earth.

Katherine's ability and willingness in the household gave Hester more time for attending to the business side of the property. But almost at once Hester, who enjoyed teaching Katherine to cook, began to avoid, whenever she could, the work of running the business. She enjoyed spinning and weaving and making clothes and, as in cooking, Katherine was quick to learn. Keeping up the ways of her grandmother Hester regularly made clothes for the children of poor families. The two of them working together were able to supply a double quantity, Katherine finding that she too loved sewing and was wonderfully neat with buttonholes and putting in zip fasteners.

They began to provide music together. Hester, peering short-sightedly at ancient copies of songs, played the piano and Katherine, who had a piping but sweet voice, sang. Often they were not in time with one another. Hester banged and crashed the keys together making the most grating discord and Katherine sang flat but neither Mr Harper nor Mr Bird, who often stayed on in the evenings, were critical.

Hester was completely happy having Katherine. She began to move more easily, swiftly even, on her English walking stick. It was imported specially having a singular gracefulness of its own, only becoming ugly, she realized, when in partnership with her own deformity. Without a stick, this stick, she was helpless. She never tried to do anything without it. She planned to herself how she would keep Katherine, perhaps travel with her sometime, educate her and leave her all her money when she died.

It had never been Hester's idea of pleasure to spend an evening at the drive-in cinema. The town boasted two which provided a repertory of extraordinarily old films. The compact little station wagon, known with reverence as 'Miss Harper's other vehicle', soon had its regular place at both. She went in the first place to please Katherine who followed the lives of certain film stars as if they were saints. Devoutly she studied magazines saving all the recent photographs. She quoted amazing facts about their marriages and their divorces, their sets of teeth, their swimming pools, their friends and about all kinds of personal details – about habits which Hester thought should have been kept private. It amused her to see Katherine adopting yet another way of speaking or of holding her head. She was influenced in some way by every film they went to. At first Hester sat with a kind of tolerance, boredom even, through long drawn-out stories which featured mainly, so the magazines said, college campus romance. They seemed to be about shrill-voiced American high-school girls competing for the affection of one special neat-footed high-school youth, also American. Since the films were American Hester could see that the characters would be American. She supposed that the stories could fit high schools in any country, but this was beyond her experience. The love affairs seemed trivial and repetitive and the songs and dances crazy, stupid and dull. Every song had its dance and both were fronted, it seemed, by increasingly bizzare heroes. Hair was longer and wilder, expressions became more vacant and guitars more ornamental. However in spite of herself and her feelings towards the films she began to find herself looking forward to the twice-weekly outings.

They were always incredibly late home after these nights. Katherine, adding fresh words and accents to her already exaggerated speech, would amuse old Mr Harper with details from the pictures and she would, the next day, encourage Hester to have what she called 'a lay in'. She took breakfast in bed to Hester and perched on the bed beside her to eat bacon and fried bread with her fingers. Often they did not really get up till lunch time. Later, as if to assert some kind of discipline, Hester would embark on a strenuous cleaning plan and would draw up programmes of work to be done by herself and Katherine. Sometimes these programmes would be torn up and burned in the kitchen stove. This burning often took the form of a little ceremony during which libations of fresh milk or wine would be poured into valuable cut glass and afterwards they would wash each other's hair with home-made infusions of rosemary.

Hester spent less and less time with her father who, like a

character in a play, wandered about the house trying to remember where his pistols were. The old man took it into his head to read cookery books ferreting them out from the backs of cupboards and shelves where Hester hid them. It became his habit to insist that chosen dishes with complicated ingredients should be prepared for him. Sometimes, late at night, he fancied a snack which entailed hours of bending over a sink under a poor light, endless shreddings and whippings and mixings and long slow cooking requiring constant stirring and watchfulness.

Hester invented ways of escaping from her father's company. She was glad when Mr Bird came and she encouraged his visits to be more frequent and prolonged into the evenings. She was still diligent in the house and the garden. She still considered the running of the property to be of first importance but she had, with her usual truthfulness, to acknowledge privately that she was not facing the responsibility most of the time and, though she tried to be as keenly interested as she had been, she knew really that she was having to force herself. As time went by, having to nurse her ailing and often demented father, she looked for small compensations. These she found more and more in teaching Katherine and in spending pleasant hours in her company.

She treated Katherine with an affectionate though severe generosity. She did not regard herself as a mother or even as an aunt. She did not attempt to give any name to the relationship. She realized quite quickly that she was possessive. She knew she was irritable and restless during the evenings if Katherine was writing a letter to one of the girls she had grown up with at the convent. And if a letter came for Katherine she always expected to be shown the contents. She told herself it was because she was fearful for the girl's well being and harmful things, like drugs, she said to herself without understanding, might come any day in the post. After all one of the girls, Hester understood from Katherine's curious language, was doing three years at the Remand. Katherine was obviously very fond of Joanna and

Hester felt guilty about her own relief that this friend was safely tucked away because of something awful she must have done; though again she had to modify this thought and understand that certain circumstances might have taken the girl to a department of rehabilitation.

They usually sat in the car outside the post office to open their letters. Katherine immediately passed over the sheets covered with round handwriting for Hester to read. The girls, she noticed, all had the same unformed or immature handwriting. They put little circles over the i's instead of dots. Often a whole page would be covered with crosses inside scrawled circles, misshapen kisses and hugs folded up into an envelope. Reassured Hester would smile and pass the pages back. She did not receive any letters herself, only bills and statements to do with the farm and requests from charities for money.

In the evenings when old Mr Harper, complaining, wanted to go over the books Hester would say, 'Later father, tomorrow, I'm busy this evening,' and would pour him an extra large whisky.

With too many hand movements and her voice going up in a self-conscious lilt at the ends of her sentences Katherine related things to Hester about the convent. She repeated several incidents of unkindness or unfair treatment often describing the same incident over again with added details which made Hester wonder sometimes about the truth of them. But true or not it was clear that were was no privacy. The beds in the long rooms were so close together that only a small chair could fit between them; and the tables in the dining room were thick with grease, and the shower room was, 'so shabby Miss Harper, dear, you can have no idea – the water never drained away so you had to stand in a slimy mess left by the other girls.' Some of the nuns were sweet, Katherine said, but others said things like they could smell that you had been thinking of a boy and that you would get pregnant as soon as you left the convent or go on drug trips and be taken away to be a prostitute. She used to dream, she told Hester, of being in the country. 'I used to pretend,' she said, 'that I had a home of my own, a farm to go to. Every night in bed I told myself stories about my family at the farm.' She smiled at Hester turning up her thin face and squinting with one eye even when the sunshine was not bright. Hester, aquainted from previous tellings, would lightly brush Katherine's thin pale hair away from her face and say, 'Well you are in the country now, and you do live on a farm. I hope you are not disappointed.' And, picturing the bleakness, she would allow some of the hidden tenderness she felt to invade her answering smile. If the squint gave her some uneasiness she dismissed it at once.

Sometimes Hester, with increasing pleasure, told Katherine stories from her own childhood, confiding details about Hilde Herzfeld about whom she had never spoken to anyone. 'She was a very strict teacher,' Hester enjoyed the recollection, 'she made me write four lines of French and four lines of German every morning before breakfast. And that was in addition to the household things my grandmother expected me to do every day.'

Late at night, when they were in their separate rooms, Hester, looking through her old albums of copied-out poems and fragments of prose carefully translated and often decorated with picture postcards, saved, or drawings made either by herself or by Hilde, wondered whether she should tell the treasured things about those times in her life. If she looked back on Hilde as Katherine must see her she noticed again, in her memories, the stains in the armpits of Hilde's dresses, *'Ach! Ich schwitze!'*, dark moist half-circles, fascinating and repelling, in the too warm stuff of which the dresses were made. Katherine with her elaborate preparations, her jars and bottles and pressure packs, her light pretty washable clothes and her scented youthful body knew nothing of these other scents. Because of things like this perhaps it would be better not to talk, better not to try to recapture something which could not exist side by side with what she had now.

She put the albums and the temporarily recalled image of Hilde's plump, often blemished, face away.

It occurred to her at night too when they had each closed their bedroom doors that Katherine, after spending an evening writing to Joanna, might go on writing to her in the privacy of her own room adding a page, or more than one, to the letter flipped to and fro with such candour in front of Hester's eyes. Hester scanning the pages of childish notepaper always said, 'That's lovely Kathy – we'll post it next time we're in town.'

While she folded back her counterpane she found herself adding to the letter as Katherine in her extraordinary idiom might. There were the frightening details extra to the descriptions of life in the convent. These details did not worry Hester, it was only the effect they could have on Katherine that mattered. There was the time Kathy and Joanna had fallen over two nuns on a mattress in a store-room. Perhaps there would be further reference to their actions, their nakedness, a glimpse of their feelings and Hester went even further – 'Imagine!' she seemed to see Katherine's blue biro labouring across a fresh sheet of paper:

'The Herzfeld chick. A TV soapy if you ask me. Big Trouble, like Sister Violetta at the Home d'ya reckon? Joanna-panna Jeez. Squeeze. Huh! eh? Makepeace and whasaname on the shed floor. Remember? Shit! Yuk! I don't hack it, but. Like Hell she musta gone for the Herzy chick. When she talks it's like *On Golden Pond* her eyes all clouded like as if these little veils of sadness come down. Wowie! Real goolish eh? Embarassing? And she packs up with whats she's on about right in the middle of a rave. The old man Jeez Joady I've told you about him. Musta made a few. Something musta happened. If I get to know!! I've seen a photo of the Herzy she's a shortie a fattie . . .'

Hester, restless in her room, thought about Katherine private in her room with her secret letter writing. She thought that Katherine would write extra things about her, laugh about her in her extra pages to Joanna.

Hester kneeling down in the narrow space beside her bed said her prayers trying to clear her mind of unprofitable thoughts and the fear of what Joanna might send back to Kathy. Her grandmother always said to have God in your heart and Jesus on your lips when you went to sleep. Ask a Blessing, she always said, and thank Him for all you've got. If you can't drop off, go on asking and thanking till you do. She must try, she told herself, not to be afraid of the friendship.

In spite of the imaginings of the night before Hester did not need much persuasion to talk again about Hilde Herzfeld. 'Fräulein she was really,' she said. 'It means Miss.' She went on to say that Hilde loved to talk about the magic of mountains and about snow and about her own little bedroom at home which had a window high up under the eaves where, in spring, the swallows nested, and where she always felt she could reach out to the mountain slope and pick up a handful of snow quite simply by leaning out of the window.

There were hotels in Europe, Hester wanted to go on telling, 'Such magnificent places, Katherine, one day I shall take you there.' She had travelled once, she said, with Fräulein Hilde. Festooned in capes and hoods and laden with trunks and baggages and packets, they had made together a sort of small Grand Tour one wonderful summer. At the hotels, Hester enjoyed remembering, everything was done to please the guests, quite elaborately at times. She remembered once a chef parading with a fanfare of trumpets and a row of prime live ducks through the hotel vestibule along a plum-coloured carpet on either side of which sat the wealthy visitors who would choose their forthcoming meal as it waddled by. Waiters stood behind every chair during the serving of afternoon tea and sang, falsetto, the correct national anthem for every guest in turn and the slices of dark fruit cake were offered with appropriate little flags piercing the moist richness. In Germany, Hester said, where they didn't know how to make tea, great trouble was taken to pour it correctly for the English from silver teapots. And for the Russians it was made with a samovar and handed to the guests in glasses cradled in little wickerwork baskets. The Russians, some of them, Hester added, held lumps of sugar between their front teeth and sucked the hot tea through the sugar. A working man's habit Miss Herzfeld had explained, rather like dipping soft white bread in coffee, but enjoyed by the rich people who, being so rich, thought they did not need to bother about manners.

'Oh, Miss Harper, dear, it would be so beautiful to travel.' Katherine sighing, patted her sewing as if to neaten it. Hester, holding up her own work to examine the stitches with a self-critical look, assured Katherine that that was what she had in mind. She went on to say that she was sure that all hotels would be the same now. One huge concrete-and-glass affair on the harbour front on Lake Ontario would be exactly the same as one in Berlin or Singapore. Waking up in any one of these places you would never be sure which country you were in. She paused and handed Katherine the large box of chocolates they were sharing. 'Try the truffles,' she said and then, arching her eyebrows, she said in an affected voice, 'Oh, for the snows of yesteryear or words to that effect.' A white rose, she said, in the bathroom one night and a red one the next would not be the same as it used to be. They would still be putting flowers in bathrooms but instead of roses and carnations misted with dew there would only be imitations. 'And everybody,' she added, freeing her teeth from a caramel, 'everybody knows how dusty plastic flowers get.' She smiled the grim little smile reserved for such comments. 'We'll have one more each and put the box away till later.' She held the box towards Katherine. 'What about a creme de menthe or a cherry liqueur,' she said shaking the box, 'but don't get it all over your sewing.' Katherine, who was, Hester knew, under the spell of a Katherine Hepburn revival (they had just seen the *African Queen* for the third time) bared her teeth in the Hepburn smile dipping her head forward then lifting it and blinking her vividly shadowed eyelids. If she had been with a man Hester would have considered her movement shamelessly flirtatious. She watched Katherine's attempts to push her cheekbones into more prominence by increasing the wideness of her smile. Hester finding the prolonged smile embarrassing and knowing the attempted provocation to be useless shook the handsome box again. 'Come on Kate,' she said, 'pick your choice,' adding impatiently, 'I can't hold these all night!'

Hester found herself thinking quite often about the film. It was not just the Hepburn mannerisms which Katherine, with such ability, copied, it was the sense of real isolation which attracted her, two people entirely alone together managing to survive and even to be happy in alien surroundings. Two people entirely alone, together and happy. A certain quality Katherine had, Hester discovered, was really quite alarming. It was almost sinister. There was nothing Katherine could not copy or learn. She seemed to have all the makings of an efficient criminal. The same qualities could go towards something more positive Hester reasoned with herself, Katherine could be an excellent business woman if necessary.

Later in the evening Katherine in a makeshift boat on the kitchen floor enacted the scene where Katherine Hepburn pours away all Humphrey Bogart's whisky. Hester, who enjoyed laughing, laughed till she ached all over.

In spite of the great difference in age and background they were able to devise entertainment for themselves. Miss Herzfeld did not come often into the conversation and Katherine did not ask questions. Hester thought the reticence would have been learned in the Orphanage.

Reading aloud they changed their voices for the different characters and laughed helplessly at their mispronouncings and mistakes. Sometimes in particularly sad and moving scenes they cried, weeping real tears, and had to comfort each other for hours.

They did not encourage visitors.

It was all simple and pleasant. Three years slipped by, the passing time hardly noticed.

One morning when bird calls were echoing across the paddocks and the air was cold and a faint mist hung over the fresh earth Mr Harper, having unsuccessfully made a partial change over to beef, died. After the death of her father Hester considered very seriously Mr Bird's suggestion that she should continue to run the property with his help. There was every chance to put right, he said, any mistakes made in recent seasons. He was, after all, her father's closest friend and, in addition, was the stock and station agent for several districts. He knew a great deal about farming and about the uses of money and he knew a great many people. He was sure, he said, that Miss Harper could manage.

Everything went well except that Hester's interest in farm management and successful sales, temporarily rekindled on complete possession of the enormous property, was shortlived. In addition, after all the years of careful frugal housekeeping, she became extravagant and wasteful. It seemed that whenever she went with Katherine to the city she had to buy everything they saw. She bought clothes, foods, furniture, cassette players and transistors. They were always needing batteries, cassettes, cooking utensils, jewellery, materials and trimmings, oil paints – for they both fancied themselves as artists – guitars – for they thought they could create a group – and they chose a new piano, Hester declaring that the terrible heat of the previous summer (a record) had warped the strings or whatever it was pianos had inside. Also Katherine coveted gear from a boutique and Italian leather boots, soft and gracefully elegant, two pairs, one pair plum coloured and the other the colour of cream on fresh milk. Hester bought too another car, this time a sturdy little truck. There was no end to their wishes and to their shopping. They were hardly ever at the farm, always on the journey to and from the city, or on the shorter journey to and from the town. They were always excited, laden with purchases and looking forward to their next expedition.

Because of driving more at night Hester had enormous bars put on the front of the Toyota. A framework of metal, a roo bar, to catch anything foolish or slow enough to be in the way in the dark on the long lonely roads. The bars were thick and strong, welded to form a sort of cage in the middle of which was a spotlight. The light had a close-fitting cover which was never taken off as Hester did not go out at night shooting.

The truck, the Toyota, was a gleaming gun-metal, severe, high off the road giving an impression of capable safety. The back was covered with a neatly fastened new tarpaulin. The cabin of the truck was comfortable being both spacious and intimate. With the bar the truck was complete and formidable. The two women enjoyed travelling in it and there was ample space for all their shopping.

Two and even more years of drought with the topsoil drifting over the fences, Mr Bird warned Hester that, if she went on the way she was, her income would become very unhealthy indeed.

One evening Mr Bird stayed later than usual. He had been obliged to put off the hired men sooner than the arranged time and was upset about this especially as he, the previous week, had had to dismiss and send away from their small houses on the property two men and their wives and children.

'Why couldn't you wait until after the harvest?' Hester demanded suddenly surprised at Mr Bird's late appearance in the kitchen and not liking his conversation.

She had always, since her earliest childhood, loved the harvest time and was happily baking scones and cakes, with Katherine's help, for the men.

'You can't afford to keep and pay men when there isn't the work,' Mr Bird began, but apparently feeling this discussion was unprofitable, he changed the subject.

'Mr Borden, you know him, young man across the paddock from you, would like to rent the big house,' he said.

'What house?' Hester's large mouth about to sample, at one bite, a jam puff, stayed wide open.

'Why this house,' Mr Bird shifted uneasily from one foot to the other before he sat down on his usual chair. 'He'd pay a good rent – he's raisin' a big family, his property adjoins, he says the house would be just what he needs. He knows you don't want to sell but would you rent . . .? It would be possible,' Mr Bird added, taking the mug of tea Hester pushed towards him, 'for you and Miss Katherine to have one of those transportable homes, very neat and new, you could have it way over by the trees, very private. The Bordens would keep to their side of the fence. Very neat and comfortable the transportables, labour saving, cut out all the polishings and repaintings that uses up your time . . .'

'Never!' Hester Harper, struggled to her feet, grabbing at her clumsy stick quickly to support herself. 'I am perfectly comfortable here, thank you, I enjoy looking after the house and the verandahs. I am used to the place. I have always lived here, it's my home.'

'It's two houses you have really,' Mr Bird ventured to remark.

'You don't need to tell me what my house is,' Hester snapped. 'It's our home.' She nodded in the direction of Katherine who, seeming not to like seeing Miss Harper upset, bent her oven-red cheeks towards the white bosom of her apron. Before there was time for further talk Hester called Katherine telling her to please show Mr Bird into the hall and out.

Mr Bird stayed away for a few days. Meanwhile Hester's busy mind during some sleepless nights (she was unaccustomed to being sleepless) was thinking things over. She was far from stupid. Mr Bird had made a point with his suggestion, she allowed this. The farmhouse was in fact two substantial houses joined by wooden verandahs; the mellow boards, she reflected, took hours of work. It was work that she loved, her life consisting always of pattern and tradition and certain ritual. The smell of linseed oil and turpentine was one of the comforts belonging to the serenity she felt when working about the house caring for polished corners and ledges. The floorboards in all the rooms gave her pleasure as did the old carpet runners and rugs. She loved thick glossy paint and enjoyed the repetitive repaintings of the walls and doors and window frames of the out-buildings. There was too the careful pleasure of washing ancient curtains, tablecloths and cushion covers alternating with an equally careful washing of antique teasets and dinner services, bowls, cups and plates and jugs and saucers, things never used but cherished as being, like the glowing furniture, part of the treasure of the old farmhouse.

The house was big and very cold in winter. Some rooms, requiring constant cleaning, were damp because they were never used. She did not want to entertain guests and certainly never now considered guests who would stay a night or several nights. She was happier simply to be alone with Katherine, just two people in a big house. Mr Bird was really right. The money from the rent, Mr Borden's rent, would lift the dwindling income. But a transportable house. 'Never!' she said aloud and, getting up early, she dressed quickly, waking Kathy quite roughly. 'Get up!' she said, 'we're going out for the day.'

An hour later they were driving in Hester's latest purchase. They drove across the paddocks so recently busy with the harvest machinery. Sheep, already feeding there, scattered and were soon hidden in the cloud of dust which accompanied the travellers.

'It's much shorter this way, dear,' Hester explained to Katherine who sat jolting on the seat clutching a hastily put-together luncheon basket from which protruded a bottle of Hester's favourite wine. She always said she could smell freshly cut grass whenever she drank it. 'We would be three times as long going round by the road,' Hester added. She explained to Katherine that there was an old cottage in the farthest corner of her land. It was a shepherd's cottage belonging to the days when men went about their work on foot or on horseback. 'No one has lived at this end of the property since I was a small child. It must be one of the most isolated places.' She smiled as if remembering something. 'If I recall properly,' she said, 'it is quite pleasing there, a lovely old woolshed, a stable, sheep pens and a poultry yard. I'm wondering what sort of condition it's in.'

The stone cottage had four rooms with little windows looking out in four directions. There was a verandah on one side and a little porch by the yard door. The only way to approach it, apart from the rough ride over the paddocks, was by a long winding track which curved sharply immediately before coming to the yard of the cottage. The saltbush on both sides of the track, they discovered when they walked a little way along it, had grown over in places but it looked as if it would be possible to drive through.

'We'll go back by the track to find out,' Hester announced. 'The Toyota,' she added, 'can get through anything.'

All the windows of the cottage were broken and the verandah was rotten but Hester declared it was all worth fixing. The landscape was stark, ugly even in its bareness. Near the boundary fence there were, at intervals, groups of trees making thin patches of shade.

Hester explained that a corner of Mr Borden's land came

down to this corner of her land. 'To get to his place,' she said, 'would take a couple of hours – but not if you head straight across the paddocks.' Katherine, who wanted to have another look inside the cottage, was not concerned about Borden's land. 'Just another quick look Miss Harper, dear. I just love the place. I could just see us sitting here at the back door. We'd make a little garden – ever so pretty.' Hester was amused, as usual, to hear a slightly different accent. She never corrected Katherine's idiom realizing that possibly life in an orphanage, a convent orphanage, might require a person to adopt a little method of defence. An accent was certainly that.

'See here, Miss Harper, dear,' Katherine was scraping at the earth, 'there's been a garden here once, you can see the edging stones.'

'Yes,' Hester said, 'and over there is an orchard.' She shaded her eyes to look across the yard at some gnarled almond trees. 'I think some of them are apricots,' she said, 'and the one nearest is an apple and right behind look like pears and quinces.' An ancient and faithful legacy, she thought, the trees might still blossom and bear fruit. It gave her pleasure to think of the planting done by an honest and hard-working shepherd who wanted to grow fruit in the time spared from tending his flocks.

Hester, looking again at the line of big trees in their groups along the boundary fence, remembered her father explaining to her once that trees growing like that suggested that there was water flowing under the earth, probably over a rock face a long way down. These old trees, he said, more than likely had their feet deep in sweet water. He said this and other things so often that Hester, long ago, stopped listening, though today she told Katherine about the trees reaching water that was often beyond the reach of men.

Across the yard at the side of the substantial shearing and woolshed was a well. It had been dry for years and was partly covered with a lid made of sections of corrugated iron fastened on to timber. The well was very wide and was built up with a coping of hand-hewn stone. The coping wall was a comfortable height for anyone wishing to sit down and rest.

Hester and Kathy sat in the sun on the wall of the well and ate their lunch and agreed readily with each other about moving out from the farmhouse and into the shepherd's cottage. They talked happily imagining how they would make a little garden, a border each with bright flowers and attractive weeds. It would be possible, they thought, to coax a little lawn and a vegetable plot. They pictured the yard alive with long-legged hens and a particularly heavy type of cat. Hester thought a rooster, a magnificent Rhode Island Red, should be included. She liked to think, she said, that he would flap his wings on the highest point of the well cover and herald the bright mornings with his crowing.

'I'll get Mr Bird to see that we have new water tanks. We'll get the run off from the house and the sheds and we'll have the poultry pens fixed and the stable door repaired. We might keep a horse.' She gave one of her loud braying laughs. 'I'll see to it all at once,' she said.

They found the gate and brought the Toyota through and, when it was time to leave, they drove back along the track which was rough but passable. Hester remarked that the drive to town would be a lot longer but they would manage she said. They would not feel lonely, she said, they had each other. All the way home Katherine chattered about red and blue checked gingham; 'so pretty for the little windows Miss Harper, dear'. Hester, listening, had her own thoughts remembering unwillingly something about loneliness. It was a memory from before Katherine came to live with her. One day the young wife of one of the farm men, dressing up her baby, had come across from the farm cottage pushing the shabby little pram over the rough ground to visit her, to talk to her and have her admire the child. Not understanding nor caring about the young mother's need, Hester had merely, from her lofty place on the verandah, dismissed the visitor watching with a superior detachment as she made her slow way back to the loneliness of the long day while her husband was somewhere out in the paddocks.

Mr Borden was pleased to pay extra rent and have the furniture which Hester said she did not need. Mrs Borden, going round the farm-house, tried to persuade Hester to take more things. She was a noisy vigorous woman and was, as always, pregnant. Certainly the house with so many rooms and the deep verandahs all round was ideal for a large family. They were accompanied during their tour by several young Bordens moving loosely in their clothes and running everywhere on thin sun-burned feet. Hester chose some of her favourite pieces of the smaller furniture. She selected china and ornaments together with most of the books which she and her father had, over the years, gathered. As soon as the cottage was ready she removed herself and Katherine and their possessions to the remote corner of the property.

The new water tanks filled with the first rains. Both women knew how to be economical with water and it did not take them long to become accustomed to kerosene lamps and a wood stove. Hester declared she liked candlelight and, surveying the wood heap, said it would attract snakes but, she added, she would kill any that showed themselves.

Hester and Katherine were comfortable together in the stone cottage. The rent money gave Hester the pleasant feeling of pocket money. She had good men working for her and Mr Bird continued to advise her.

Often she felt she did not need advice. She had the reputation of being a quick-witted business woman, quite hard headed, they said at the sales. She understood the rain clouds, the east wind, the movements of the sun and the varying conditions of the soil. Water, she told Katherine, moves unexpectedly and the changing colour from one end of a paddock to the other tells you where the water is and how far down it is. For some years she had been resting on her reputation and her knowledge and she continued without thinking much about it to do so.

Mr Bird called at intervals. One day, taking Hester on one side, he warned her in a roundabout way not to trust any person too completely. 'Any person, Miss Hester,' he said, 'as you are not acquainted entirely with, I mean, what's in their lives, what's gone before and such.' Not noticing Hester's increasingly stormy frown he continued, 'You being good hearted don't have the knowing of the bad sides of people.' Irritated, Hester told him to mind his own business and to confine his remarks to the running of the farm. 'What I am saying concerns just that,' he said in a low voice. They were walking cross the yard near the old well.

'Well cover's a bit loose Miss Hester,' he changed the subject as they paused between the disused woolshed and the well. Once more Hester told him not to interfere. The well she said was useless and was nothing to do now with the farm and whether the cover was repaired or not was her own private affair. She said she hoped that Mr Bird would not raise either subject again.

The well had become for Hester and Katherine a place where they liked to sit sunning themselves. On bright hot days, where they could see a little way into it, the inside of the well seemed cool and dark and tranquil. Mysterious draughts of cold air seemed to come from somewhere deep down in the earth. If they bent their heads close to the unclosed part of the cover they thought that, even though the well was dry, they could hear from its depths the slow drip drop of water.

Hester even thought she could smell water but dismissed the thought, knowing that there could not be any. Some days the wind sang in the empty well shaft and, on other days, their voices seemed to echo and reverberate as they sat together on the generous coping talking to and fro contentedly to one another.

Inside the well going down into the blackness were stout

metal rungs. This ladder of spaced-out rungs was set firmly into the structure of the well. The rungs were very close to the stone work and anyone climbing up or down would have to place the toes of his boots carefully and rely on being able to hold the rungs above. It was clear too that it would be impossible to avoid grazing the knuckles on both hands, first one and then the other, as the hands grasped the rungs, one after the other, either going down or coming up.

Hester explained to Katherine that the rungs went only a short way down, not much more than the height of a tall man and then it was a sheer drop. She did not know, she said, why the rungs were there and, being there, she did not know why they did not go all the way down. She thought that perhaps at one time the water had been up to the lowest rung.

Sometimes they threw small stones into the well and though they sometimes hit the sides of the shaft they never heard them reach the bottom.

Hester often threw broken or badly burned dishes down the well. She had come, she said, to disliking spending too much time on washing up. 'There's a fortune,' she said, 'in bits of antique crockery down there.'

To amuse themselves they pretended that someone lived in the well. A troll with horrible anti-social habits had his home down in the depths. They invented too an imprisoned princess, the possession and plaything of the troll. She was later changed to a prince as Katherine felt it would be more exciting and 'more *trewly* romantic Miss Harper, dear,' if a prince on a white horse came out from the well one fine day.

'Oh yes, instead of a princess,' Hester readily joined in, 'who would require looking after and who would only mess up the bathroom with her endless cosmetics. The prince,' she agreed, 'would be more useful about the place and a horse, especially a thoroughbred, would be lovely!' There was the stable with the door open all ready . . . She laughed.

'Oh Miss Harper, dear,' Katherine said, 'how would we get the horse up?'

'We'd have to use the block and tackle.' Hester turned her head to regard the ancient equipment which jutted on a rusty railing from the end of the old shed; high up in a position of once-held power.

'The prince,' Katherine said, 'must be taller than me.'

'Than I,' Hester, as was her habit, corrected. 'Taller than I am Kathy,' she said.

'Yes, taller than yew Miss Harper, dear,' Katherine said. 'Men should always be tall, the man should always be taller than the woman.'

'Yes,' Hester agreed, feeling it right that the man should be tall, taller than the woman, but knowing that once again she had failed to make the grammatical point.

'And older,' Katherine persisted.

'Oh yes,' Hester again agreed though knowing that in the farmyard young roosters, smaller then the hens, mated with their own sisters, mothers and grandmothers. She reflected on Naomi asking her daughters-in-law if they wanted to wait until she bore more sons. She, for a moment, tried to consider the stick-like limbs of the newly born boys in their cradles, it would never be possible to offer these to the fecund bodies of the two youthful and possibly buxom widows. She felt sure, she said, dismissing the ancient mixture of manipulation and devotion, that the troll would be the best person to haul up from the bottom of the well. 'Imagine!' she said, 'how easily he would carry the firewood indoors on his bent back. I don't suppose your prince, however tall, would want to spoil his white velvets.'

Katherine, sighing, replied that she supposed she would have to sit up nights sewing overalls for him.

In the winter, when it was cold, they did not think of the well. The mechanical rhythmic rattling of the iron cover on windy nights had a soothing quality rather like the sound of a big clock ticking when one is accustomed to the gentle regularity. Certainly in winter the stone coping did not invite them. They kept within doors, burning wonderful fires, cooking good meals and eating them and enjoying their reading and sewing and their home-made music and singing.

Sometimes Hester ordered clothes and patterns and materials from big shops in the city but ordinarily they drove into the town for provisions. Because of tourists, the town having buildings which were described as splendid reminders of the past and, because of city people caught in the everlasting dream of going back to the land and being wealthy enough to take up small parcels of sub-divided land, the town had an air of being busy with a pleasant market-day atmosphere.

Mrs Grossman, taking advantage, had enlarged the stock in her general store to include axe heads and mattock handles, hats with wide brims and fly veils and those relics which people like to have as ornaments on their recently acquired properties; things like brightly painted, metal-bound cart and carriage wheels, milk churns, ancient and now illegal rabbit traps and battered discarded road signs. She had taken over the empty butcher's shop next door (the other side from the hotel), and she quickly filled the window with cracked vegetable dishes, cruets, gravy boats, empty sauce and pickle bottles, black iron kettles, black preserving pans – too heavy to lift, wooden wash tubs and candle sticks of brass. She even had some knives and forks of the sort which need cleaning daily and she had the butcher's chopping block freshly salted and scrubbed and priced. Some enthusiast would be sure to want it in her kitchen. She hoped too to get a couple of pews from the Holy Trinity Anglican Church, it being declared in a handbook as one of the oldest churches in existence. People, it seemed, liked to sit in pews for a barbecue. Very fitting, Mrs Grossman said, since barbecues were often on a Sunday.

At the convent, Katherine told Miss Harper, there was a one-armed woman who did the ironing, not all of it as the girls did ironing every day, and this woman had a boyfriend who, one night in a fit of pique, cut off the other arm – it seemed because of her only having one arm – making her less attractive than ever.'She bled something awful Miss Harper, dear, out by the toilets there she was in a pool of blood. They said he hanged himself after cutting off his own arms.'

The journey into town provided a time for the retelling of items from old newspapers which, as time went on, became legends, believed by them both. The town was not large. Hester knew the district well and though she could not quote the population she knew how many head of cattle every farmer owned. She was sympathetic to misfortune and helped a great many people but itinerant workers bowed down with personal tragedy she refused to have on her property, saying quite bluntly that she had to prosper and would only be held back by the down and out and the feckless.

As they crossed the road bridge into the town Hester would always remark on the low level of water in the river which lay very still and wide far down beneath the long bridge. The bridge was the entrance to the town and it was also the way of escape from the town. Hester, without fail, felt an excitement as she drove on to the bridge to start the homeward journey.

For years the river had been low. 'Needs a good flushing out,' Mrs Grossman said repeatedly in an accusing tone as if some weekend customer was to blame. A newcomer, one of the new hobby farmers on five useless acres of salt flat, timidly asked Mrs Grossman for a square plastic bowl so that her husband could wash his feet. 'My husband is a bank manager,' she explained.

'They don't come square,' Mrs Grossman replied, still preoccupied with the state of the river as if Miss Harper, with the power of the large land owner, could alter it. A creek in a deep ravine on the western side of Hester's land fed the river. In summer the pits and gullies in the creek bed were dry but when the rain came water flowed swiftly rising and flooding in a few minutes, only to recede as quickly. Hester, though she did not bother to tell Mrs Grossman, thought that the water must flow away in underground streams. Sometimes during the very hot dry weather she wished she could reach this good water which was somewhere a long way down under the earth pouring itself away, wasted.

Mrs Grossman never kept Miss Harper waiting in the shop. Sometimes Mr Grossman and Mrs Grossman together attended to Miss Harper's needs and carried her shopping out to her car and then stood respectfully in the street leaving the other customers in the shop waiting till Hester had taken off with a roar in the direction of the bridge.

'You ought to keep a coupla dogs,' Mr Bird, refusing to learn from previous experience, advised one day when he brought a parcel which had come by rail to his office in town. 'Your father, Miss Hester, always had dogs,' he said. 'Never was seen without a bluey or a red cloud at his side. You would do well to do likewise.'

'Yes I know,' Hester pretended to dash a tear from the side of her long nose. 'Poor father!' she said. 'Of course I shall never forget his dogs.'

Hester had no intention of keeping a dog. 'It's too much work feeding them,' she said to Katherine almost before Mr Bird's dust had settled. 'I don't care if we are alone here,' she said. 'Dogs don't save people if strangers come. They often fawn on the most sinister-looking individuals.' She went on to describe how a dog she'd known of jumped in the truck being stolen by thieves and went off for the ride. 'And,' she added, 'they bark madly in the night, so that you think someone's prowling round in the dark. In any case, before the end I got heartily stick of father's dogs. Father got that his dogs had fillet steak every day while the rest of us could live on boiled wheat for all he cared. And do you remember how we had to chop up celery and lamb's fry for

Floss? That disgusting old hearth rug. What a mess she made everywhere. I know it wasn't her fault really but we simply couldn't go through that again!' They both forgot the advice about a dog and took the parcel indoors.

There were geese about the place and Hester knew that an intruder might well be frightened of the flock. There were four white ganders with strong flexible necks. They were powerful birds and their blue eyes were cold and steady. In any case she knew she could protect herself and Kathy. She had a gun somewhere. She was not sure now where it was. It was bound to be somewhere; mislaid, she thought, during the move. She meant to find it and put it on top of her wardrobe but in an uncharacteristic way, she let the gun and its much-needed meticulous care slip from her mind.

They tore off the crackling wrapping papers as soon as they were in the house and quickly tried on the new underclothes and the slippery silky nightgowns Hester had ordered for them. With little yelps and screams of excitement they paraded, Hester on her stick heavily, in front of some new full-length mirrors purchased a few weeks earlier. Since they were so far from any other dwelling they could make as much noise as they liked. Hester, when really roused and excited, was capable of making sounds like a fog-bound ship knowingly approaching a rocky harbourless coast. This night she brayed like an enthusiastic donkey.

'Oh my dear!' she gasped between a series of long drawn-out fog horns. *'Pour une femme troublante, passionée – sophistiquée!* What a splendid label!' Her fingers ran crookedly up and down the piano keys as she fumbled for a tune, and Katherine, crooning, swaying her hips and clicking her fingers, modelled the new clothes. She paced forward and, swinging round, she posed. She froze, legs and arms caught in the middle of a movement, completely still, transparent like long icicles faintly rosy, apricot coloured, as if formed from water dripping slowly over a rusty gutter. Several times she went through this little intimate routine displaying the feathery black fragments of clothing, taking them off and putting them on and, sometimes, pausing to fold or to unfold each item carefully with little thoughtful twists and shakings.

'And now the little corset,' Hester said crashing a drum roll on the bass notes, hitting several at once. Turning from the pages of the music at which she peered closely because of her short sight she smiled with approval at Kathy's practised contortions.

They enjoyed the evening thoroughly. Hester, though she scarcely admitted it, found that she looked forward to evenings of this sort and, in particular, to Katherine's dancing.

Between them they developed a capacity for pleasure. Their life was all pleasure. The yard was well stocked with poultry. Hester declared often that she never felt so comfortable as when a sack of laying pellets, in the back of the old station wagon, slipped and pressed against the seat as if offering to support her in the small of her back. Sometimes this reassurance caused her to give a little half-hidden sigh. She liked poultry she said because they did not require anyone to supply a life for them as dogs and people did. 'Poultry,' she said, 'enjoy your company if you're prepared to give it, but if you don't want to bother you can just throw them their food and forget about them.' She went on to say that it did not do to spoil farm animals. 'Take cats,' she said, 'cats need to be treated fairly but it's a mistake to make a fuss of them.' They now had three thin but heavily built cats of a greyish colour. All had characteristic tabby rings patterning their dusty fur. The cats were not encouraged to come into the house.

Sometimes Hester sat with the poultry noticing in her mind which bird would be the best to knock off next for a good meal. With the shiny toe of her black orthopaedic boot she stroked a nearby cat and narrowed her eyes in the direction of an exceptionally greedy and plump white duck. She maintained that a little personal notice did not do any harm and that it was possible to encourage eggs from hens and ducks at times when they seemed lonely or depressed.

Both women were very fond of roast duck and usually ate one between them once a week.

The delightful thing about Katherine was that she grabbed life with both hands. She wanted all the life as she saw it in films. She wanted adventure and Hester was drawn into this wanting. It took many forms, one of them being having everything that money can buy. Advertisements everywhere, in magazines and especially at the cinema, told Katherine that if only she had this or that perfect happiness would be hers. Hester's common sense deserted her quite often and, without meaning to be, she was taken in.

They collected innumerable cookery books. The more exotic titles attracted them and they enjoyed selecting dishes that contained things they did not have in the house. Hester who, in previous years, would never have made an extra trip to town if she found she had forgotten something now made journeys when some small item was required. Paprika for instance or a small quantity of soft brown sugar. They spent hours preparing piquant orange and plum sauces for roast ducklings. Hester, coating the succulent servings with a remarkable glaze, felt that she was doing justice to the creatures she had reared. They made variations on salad dressings with thinly sliced avocado pears, crushed garlic and black olives. Hester's favourite book of recipes was called *My Friend The Garlic Crusher*.

The wood stove had an excellent oven. When the potatoes, roasted in their jackets, were carried to the table, golden brown, soaked in butter and decorated with chopped chives, Hester declared in that famous old cliché that they were out of this world. She even imitated, not very well, Katherine's American accent. Their simple little dinners were often a work of art. They developed too the habit of having a glass of champagne each with their sodden cornflakes at breakfast.

Between them, Hester because of her lame leg mainly giving orders, they made the little garden. The imagined vegetable plot, the little lawns and the two borders, one each, with flowers and attractive weeds, came to life.

Sometimes, though not very often they thought about the outside world. They, feeling that they had eaten too heavily would walk a little way along the overgrown track in order to digest their big meal and then, coming indoors, Hester would write one or two small cheques to send to worthy organizations who were preventing the populations of poverty-stricken countries from starving to death. On these occasions, acting on Hester's instructions, Katherine would bring several armfuls of clothes from their respective bedrooms and spread them on the sofa and the chairs and then they would go over the clothes trying to decide which things they no longer wanted. This was difficult to do for as soon as Katherine said her pink dress was really out of fashion and too childish now Hester would cry, 'But darling Kathy! Not your little pink! I remember so clearly the day we chose it. You must keep it always! For ever!' And when Hester, with a flamboyant gesture, gathered into a cardboard box whole heaps of her own garments Katherine wept and said that Miss Harper would surely freeze in the winter, wasn't it all her good woollens she was giving away. Some hours would pass like this and , in the end, tired but triumphant, they would reach a decision which satisfied them both and a smallish parcel would be made of some unwanted articles of clothing to be sent to the Home which was how Katherine always spoke of the Orphanage. The dinner dishes, cold and greasy, remained on the table and in the kitchen sink till the next morning. Any dish which proved too disgusting to clean was simply carried outside and pushed through the hole in the rotting corrugated-iron cover of the well.

For some years Hester had regularly sent money to the family of a needy child rescuing it from starvation and, apparently, her cheques were educating it. Sometimes she tried to remember how long this had been going on. The child, she thought it was a boy, in some far-away country, sent little letters and photographs at intervals through an organization distributing the funds.

One day sitting in the chunky little Toyota outside the post office in town Hester, rifling eagerly through her mail which consisted mainly of bills and advertisements, tore open an envelope containing another little letter and a photograph. As though struck for the first time by an enlightening thought she said, 'You know, Katherine, I declare it's all of ten years since I took on this boy, I would have preferred a girl naturally, and look at this photograph, he is still the same size as he was ten years ago. Also his handwriting has not changed.' She peered with a disagreeable expression at the contents of the letter. 'I shall not send any more money,' she said. 'He should be old enough now to be earning his own living.'

After their dinner that night Hester, who had been brooding, relented and, loosening the hooks on her ample skirts, she limped to the dresser where, with her scratchy pen, she wrote out a cheque. 'Put this in an envelope, Kathy,' she said. 'The letter and the photograph could well be from a younger brother or sister. They all look alike don't they and they have such enormous families, these deprived people.' Katherine did as she was told insisting that Miss Harper was truly the most generous person she had ever known.

'Trewly Miss Harper, dear,' she crooned, 'the mostest generous person Ah ever done knowed, yew trewly air!'

Later in the evening noticing that Katherine seemed very quiet, subdued even, Hester, looking up from her sewing, asked her what the matter was. Was she not feeling well, she wanted to know. When Katherine did not answer but simply bent lower over her own sewing, Hester patted the sofa. 'Come and sit by me,' she said, 'and tell me what the matter is.' She moved along to make more room. She thought she could see tears on Katherine's cheeks, and now they were sitting close she saw and felt them. She brushed Katherine's hair back from her face with a clumsy but tenderly intended movement.

Not used to keeping anything back from Miss Harper, Katherine confessed that she had not shown the letter she received that morning. Miss Harper, she said, had been busy with her own mail and she had kept her letter hidden. It was from Joanna who was now out. It was not prison really, Katherine explained, only a place to get better from 'what she'd been taking Miss Harper, dear, she's the sweetest most lovely person Miss Harper, dear, I know you'd love her.'

'Was there anything in with the letter?' Hester, wanting to know, was unrestrained and direct.

Katherine was shocked. 'Oh no Miss Harper, dear,' she said. She pulled the little childish pink pages out of her pocket. 'Here it is, of course you can read it Miss Harper, dear.'

Hester did not take long to read the letter, the handwriting was so big there were not many words on the page. It seemed that Joanna was wanting more than anything in the whole world to see Katherine. A whole page of kisses and hugs endorsed this apparently innocent wish. Katherine watching Miss Harper read began to cry again.

'For heaven's sake! Katherine there's nothing to cry about,' Hester said, trying not to let her voice show that the letter caused her to feel threatened and afraid.

'But,' Katherine sobbed, 'I, I hope you won't mind, Miss Harper, dear, I want to see Joanna too. Only we're so far away from each other. As you see she's got a place to live . . . in that hostel and . . . and she's got a job, the typing job.'

'Well,' Hester said, 'that's as it should be. She couldn't go back to the convent at her age.' She was trying to be very sensible. 'And it's very good that she's been given the chance. There's nothing to cry about, now is there!'

'Sometimes,' Katherine sobbed, 'I wish for, wish for . . .'

'Company of your own age?' Hester, trying again, was hiding the fact that she was very much shaken, 'It's very natural that you should wish for young people and especially for, for Joanna,' the name came out in an artificial tone, 'since you grew up together and must feel like, feel, feel –

feel – like sisters – almost.' Even as she spoke Hester felt a kind of petulance. She had no idea that Katherine was not perfectly content. She felt increasingly a mixture of hurt and annoyance as well as fear. This friendship carried a threat; things read about in newspapers. She wished that the girl had tried to escape and been caught and kept in with her sentence doubled. 'Good Behaviour,' Joanna had written in her little pink letter, 'what a laugh! Here I am out before time, but.' The writing paper was wickedly innocent. Hester would have liked to screw it up into a tight ball and burn it. Annoyance made her tremble. Hadn't she, Hester Harper, grown up entirely with her grandmother and her father and a few farm workers for company. Apart from the time when Hilde Herzfeld was there and the two years at the boarding school she had spent all her life on the farm. Why then, the bitter voice inside her persisted, was Katherine so ungrateful. She, Hester, was sure she was doing everything possible to make a happy life for Katherine, a happy life, she thought, for them both. Suddenly she felt terribly unhappy and afraid that her anger would show itself. Her head throbbed; she hoped she was not going to have one of her bad headaches. She wondered if all the affection had been purely on her side. Restraining herself, for she would have liked to shake Katherine, she put an arm round the girl's shoulders.

'Come along!' she said as cheerfully as she could. 'If you don't mind sharing your bedroom, as we don't have much space here, why don't you answer your letter now and invite Joanna for a few days or a week. Yes, perhaps a week? Would that make you happy?' Hester was aware that her voice was self conscious and gruff. As she spoke she wished she was not saying the things she was saying. Immediately she pictured the two girls endlessly together, perhaps laughing about her behind her back; talking in low voices in their room at night – with the door closed so that she would hear their voices, intimate, with little bursts of mirth and affection from which she would be excluded. The week would be unbearably long, but she had said it now.

'Oh Miss Harper, dear!' Katherine exclaimed. 'Oh could I?'

'Yes, yes of course Kathy,' Hester said. 'I insist you write at this moment.' A kind of wisdom invaded her and she felt grateful to herself that she had had the sense to suggest inviting only one girl. 'I, of course,' she said, 'will pay the return train fare and we can drive to town to meet the train.'

'Oh thank you Miss Harper, dear! How simple it all sounds when you talk about it.' Katherine, not realizing that Hester was thinking in terms of a ticket valid for one week only, leaned her flushed face against Hester's stiff black sleeve. 'Thank you Miss Harper, dear.' She had stopped crying at once. Hester did not need to pat her shoulder and say, 'there there' over and over again. She did pat the shoulder, awkwardly, once and, reaching for her stick, she struggled to her feet. The low sofa made the struggle necessary. Usually she sat on an upright wooden chair.

In the kitchen Hester, conscious of her shaking hands, failed to light the primus stove even at a second attempt and the kitchen was filled with kerosene fumes. Katherine, at once, took over the lighting of the stove in a most natural way either not noticing or pretending not to notice. Hester leaned against the door post and watched with Katherine as the blue flames roared under the little tin kettle they used when they wanted tea in a hurry.

During the night Hester, who felt very tired, was wakeful. It seemed to her that after sleeping heavily she was no longer able to sleep and her right arm felt numb. She recalled, as she lay awake trying to feel confident that she was able to move her arm and that it was only pins and needles because of lying on the arm while she was asleep, that she had been very tired lately. Her other knee seemed weak and at times when she was stepping up a step it almost seemed as if the knee on her good leg was not able to take the weight thrown on to it because of the weakness and awkwardness of the lame leg. She wondered if she could have had a mild stroke. This thought was so alarming, the thought of Katherine all alone and herself unable to speak or to move, that she raised herself up and getting out of bed she walked as firmly as she could about her small bedroom. There was no sound from Katherine's little room opposite.

Quietly Hester closed her door and, finding the matches she lit her candle. It was with relief that she found herself able to do these things. She was perfectly all right, after all, she told herself. And, with her usual honesty, she went on to tell herself that she was jealous. Actually jealous. At her age. All because Katherine wanted the company of this Joanna. Rubbish company, a girl who could do nothing but harm. Hester was vague in her mind about the life this other girl could have had but it was dirty and infected and should be kept away from the freshness and purity of their own lives. She tried to think of other things. Thinking of her endless paddocks should comfort her. She loved her land but recently had been forced to realize that the years of drought had now become several years. She was relieved that Mr Borden still wanted to live in the farmhouse. She never went across there. Days, weeks, months, years with Katherine made time go by very quickly. The farmhouse seemed a long way away.

That Katherine could have such a wish, Hester reasoned, was natural. She kept telling herself this but such reason did not help her. She dreaded the hovering loneliness.

She thought, in spite of loving the farm, how intolerable the black moonless nights in the wheat would be if she had all her days and nights alone. Katherine might well, she shivered at the idea, be tempted by Joanna's stories of her own life to want to leave. The quiet secluded old woman's life, for that is how it could be described, was not really the desired thing for a young woman like Katherine.

She found herself, without explanation, poking about in one of the cupboards in her room. One of the things she pulled out to study carefully in the soft light of her candle was an old photograph of herself when she was a little girl. A photograph taken by a professional photographer in a shop.

She had not looked at the photograph for years and now

suddenly all sorts of memories of fondness and cherishing came back to her. Suddenly she wanted to be Hetty, the little lamb, Hetty, my lamb, again. She could, as she looked, almost feel the crêpe de chine of the new frock on her bare legs. The blue and fawn pattern was there in the picture. Now she remembered it clearly, the clinging material very soft and light. It was as though she could, even now, feel the white-ribbed silk socks tight round her legs. When she looked at the polished leather sandals she felt as if she possessed them and wore them still, so vividly did they come back to her from the picture.

The photograph was tinted, professionally, so that she had, as was thought pretty then for a little girl, a rosy pursed-up little mouth and rounded cheeks the colour of ripe peaches. Looking closely for several minutes she recalled the voices from her childhood and knew that she did not hear them, only longed to hear them as she was, without acknowledging it, longing to be cherished again in the way she once had been by her father and her grandmother and, for a few years, by Hilde Herzfeld. A rush of remembered fondness for her grandmother was like a pain. This pain was followed quickly by another as she thought of her father. Latterly, before he died, she was always escaping from him as he became more of an invalid and an increasingly tiresome bore. Sure, she said to herself then, to drive even sheep away. Only Mr Bird was faithful perhaps because of being such a bore himself he did not notice. But as a child she accompanied him everywhere, her little crutch dot dotting fast to keep up with his long stride. In those far off days she wore a red woollen hat knitted by her grandmother. This hat with its tassel Hester still had. She still used it, darned several times, as her father used it after it was considered too childish for her. Like her father she kept her money in it. Bank notes and change, often a great deal, rolled up, hidden in the soft wool and placed on the top shelf of the kitchen dresser next to the spikes for bills and receipts, the cheque book and the pen and ink. Hester paid for everything with cash, keeping the cheque book for distant payments, the city shops and the selected few charities which, fortunately, did not have to survive on her meagre contributions.

Hester had never known her mother. Neither had Katherine. They did not talk of this as the word seemed to have very little meaning for either of them. Katherine, lacking a father too, had quickly learned while Hester's father was alive how to behave with him, how to answer him and when to avoid him. She was very adaptable Hester noticed at once. She thought this was probably because of the kind of people she had had to be with at the orphanage.

The lame leg had not shown on the photograph even though the low-waisted dress was short. The skilful photographer had arranged her to sit in such a way that the little body and limbs looked perfect, the lame foot was tucked in behind the good one. Perhaps that was why, when she became older and painfully aware of the disfigurement, she had removed the photograph from its place and put it away. Perhaps her father realizing the reason had refrained from mentioning the disappearance of the touched-up little Hester. Or, as she rebuked herself now in this long night for taking out the photograph, perhaps he had never noticed that the picture had gone from its accustomed place. Nothing could have covered the pale space left on the wall because it had been in the sitting room, or drawing room as her grandmother called it, where it would not have been possible to pin up one of the poultry-feed or farm machinery calendars they received every year.

Hester's headache was accompanied by that total lack of dignity suffered during bouts of vomiting, not once or twice but several times, first undigested food, of which she was deeply ashamed and then painfully and with difficulty, bile. She wanted to tell Katherine how dreadfully sorry she was about it all but she could only groan and keep her eyes closed. She felt Katherine's small hands as they patted her forehead gently and she felt the cold compresses which were dutifully laid across her pain. Katherine kept the room dark and emptied the basin repeatedly as she had learned to do during previous headaches. Bilious attacks, Hester called them if she had to explain an absence to anyone.

'What time is it,' Hester managed to ask in a weary voice in the darkened room.

'Why Miss Harper dear, it's four o'clock. Should you feel like some tea and toast?' Katherine, who was sitting by the bed, stood up and leaned over, smoothing the sheet and the pillow and Hester's hair with her cool little hands.

'No thank you Kathy,' Hester said. She felt weak and tired and tearful. 'I'll try and sleep. You go out in the air a bit. You can't sit by me all day.'

The headache lasted two days. Hester felt the pain go away during the afternoon of the second day. She lay in the bed hardly daring to move. Tears of relief squeezed out from the corners of her eyes and spilled, trickling down her cheeks. How sweet and kind Katherine always was during this recurring nuisance. She must be feeding the poultry, it was the kind of noise she could hear now from the yard.

As she felt better thoughts and words formed in her mind. She thought about grass, the west paddock by the farm-house came right up to the bedroom windows which opened like narrow doors on to the verandah. At a certain time of the year the grass was rich and sweet smelling. She thought about the word meadow, a grassy paradise – someone had written that about a meadow. Somewhere in her childhood reading there were daisy chains and butter-cups and the idea of crawling through a hole in a hedge into some magic place, a meadow it was called, deep with long grass and yellow flowers. Hester, for a moment, recalled her father and thought of him dismissing the flowers, cape weed, with disgust. Grass, she remembered more words in the spreading freedom as the pain seemed to be lifted from her brow; *a fragrant garment of the earth filled with ripe summer to the edge*. And more words; *all spring and summer is in the fields silent scented paths*. Was that

Ruskin she wondered. She had all these words copied out in her neat schoolgirl writing. Some lines were even translated into French and German, Fräulein Herzfeld made her translate everything . . .

No headache at all now. She tried to remember where the apostrophe in *fields* should go.

'It doesn't matter,' she said aloud and was startled by her own voice, 'there are only two possible places. Katherine!' she called, 'Katherine!', knowing that her voice could not be heard over the raucous insane cackling from the yard. 'Katherine!'

But Katherine heard and came. 'Yes, Miss Harper, dear?'

'Kathy. I think I could take some tea now, very weak and no milk.'

'Oh yes, Miss Harper, dear, of course I'll make it at once.'

Joanna replied to the invitation, accepting it, and at once they began suitable preparations for the visit. Joanna's letter, decorated with *Snoopy* and the paper made to look like denim, lay on the corner of the dresser. It was impossible while passing not to look at the letter; the large unformed handwriting was compelling, it seemed full of life and the expectation of happiness. From time to time Katherine picked up the letter and re-read it though she must have known its contents by heart. Hester noticing the quick re-readings bit her lip and said nothing. It seemed to her that the pages of the letter had a sweet heavy scent, something powerful which she could not define. Sometimes she thought Katherine smelled like the letter but perhaps that was because she was so often holding it. Hester could not bring herself to speak about it. She had read once, in a magazine, an article, a heart-breaking article about a mother detecting drugs used by her daughter because she, the mother, had noticed a smell: The awful part was that the mother's nose had been too slow and the daughter had gone blind. When discussing the article with

Katherine at the time, Katherine, assuming an air of importance, had said that she knew a lot of people who were stoned wild regularly and not one of them was blind or had anything wrong with them at all. 'Perhaps the lady is a foreign lady Miss Harper, dear,' she said. 'They write awful stuff in places like England and America to scare the kids.'

But Hester, holding the scent of the letter in her large nose, was not at all sure.

Joanna's visit was still a little time off as she was in a typing pool and had to wait for her appointed holiday. The letter on the dresser caused a small deep frown to appear at the fleshy bridge of Hester's nose. Since she did not look in the mirror at moments like this she had no idea how much more severe the frown made her look.

One morning while they were eating an early breakfast Hester, suddenly disturbed by the too close crowing of their most handsome rooster, tilted her chair back and, putting an arm round the edge of the flywire door, caught the bird by the neck and, with a twist of her strong fingers, she broke his neck.

'Oh Miss Harper, dear,' Katherine began.

'Hang him up in the shed, Katherine,' Hester said going on with her meal. 'We'll deal with him later. A good dinner!' she laughed her loud braying laugh. 'In mid-crow,' she said. 'He's been getting on my nerves lately.'

Hester knew she could not ask Katherine about the scent on the letter, the pages still smelled or seemed to smell. What could Katherine say to any question about the scent of a letter. I don't notice anything Miss Harper, dear, or, in one of her film-star voices, oh Miss Harper, dear, it's my perfume. Remember the French perfume spray, *Chloe*, you bought me? I've just started to use it. Joanna will love it. She'll rave about it.

But Katherine was talking, 'We'll be able, Joanna and me . . . we'll be able to go to town in our gear.'

Hester was too slow to correct as she usually did. 'We'll be able, Miss Harper, dear, to wear our boots in town. I've always felt too shy to wear them going out but with Joanna,' she paused, 'it'll be just great, but. The only trouble is . . .' Katherine said, 'how will we get to town from here. I mean how shall we get to the café . . .'

'I shall drive you there of course,' Hester's reply was prompt. They looked at each other across the table. Katherine's expression suggested a dismay which she was attempting to conceal. Hester, seeing herself through the eyes of Katherine and Joanna when they were together, imagined herself sitting like a poker, a black one, at one of the laminex tables, probably one with a messy top, while the two girls, overdressed and self conscious in their high boots, put coins in the juke box at the same time eyeing the few youths and tossing their heads at the stringy-haired country girls who would also be eyeing the heroes of the wheat as they gathered in their one meeting place, the road house, *El Bandito*.

'Oh Miss Harper, dear, you couldn't,' Katherine whispered.

'I could wait in the car,' Hester said with her grim little smile.

'I could take my sewing with me and sit in the car.'

'Oh Miss Harper, dear, you couldn't!' Katherine cried. 'I wouldn't hear of such a thing.' She paused. 'Miss Harper, dear,' she said, 'could I learn to drive? Please?'

'Perhaps,' Hester began with reluctance. Remembering her sick headache she tried not to be too grudging. 'I'll think about it,' she said.

It was more than possible, she was thinking, that Joanna could drive. She was able, in her mind, already able to hear Joanna's voice calling: 'All right if we take the car Miss Harper? O.K. if we have the car tonight Miss Harper? We'll need the car, Miss Harper, all day.' My car, Hester said to herself, her frown deepening. Katherine, now busy at the sink, did not see Hester's face. 'Hurry up with those dishes, Katherine,' she said, 'if you must drive, you must! We'll go out today, straight away.'

'Oh thank you Miss Harper, dear, thank you. I'll get my

test first pop, you'll see! Give me five minutes and I'm finished here.' Katherine washed and dried the last dishes while Hester limped out into the yard where she stood waiting, unwilling and wooden, beside the Toyota.

Mr Bird called to see Hester. His visit was sooner than expected. Hester preferred to have the farm discussion at specific times and she usually arranged these times to suit herself. An enormous tea drinker, Mr Bird sat to drink tea with them. He was, Hester said privately to Katherine in the kitchen while they were splitting scones and spreading them with strawberry jam and cream, quite kind but an utter bore. She often felt, she said, like screaming with boredom when he was there. She did not scream however. A recurring painful memory prevented any showing of hysterical or true feelings. It was not so long ago that time could blur entirely a farm-management conversation when Mr Bird had come directly to the point and warned Hester that with the death of her father she would become a very well-to-do woman and that there was always the possibility that some man, out for land and money, might make up to her with a view to marriage. He had spoken as gently as he could but the very truth that he uttered was one which Hester knew and understood all too well; the awful fact that a man, if one should come, would not want her in her ugliness for herself but want her only as a means to the possession of her land.

'I think and have always thought,' Mr Bird added more pain in his meant kindness, 'that you are a handsome woman Miss Hester and very clever too but there's those I would protect any woman from.'

'Thank you, Mr Bird,' Hester said then, 'I have absolutely no intention of marrying anyone.' Later in the privacy of her bed she had been unable to stop a terrible bitter silent weeping because any tiny hope seemed to have gone completely. She had in her room chests packed with household linen embroidered during the years with Miss Herzfeld. Laughingly in drawn-thread work and with generous smooth stitching, white upon white, the two of them had initialled sheets, table cloths, table napkins, little linen towels and pillow slips with an elaborate monograph designed from a double aitch Hilde Herzfeld and Hester Harper or Harper and Herzfeld. Miss Herzfeld, making her way into the youthful Hester's heart, taught her to wash her neck every day with cold water so that it would be beautiful to receive, when the time came, the necklaces and pendants and jewels some man would want to cherish her with. Both of them had washed their necks religiously even on the coldest mornings with the coldest water.

So Miss Harper did not scream. As she told herself on other occasions, when she managed to dismiss Mr Bird's intimate conversation, she also had a respect for her father's money and needed advice so that she and Katherine could spend and enjoy themselves without reducing themselves to poverty. She needed Mr Bird and, when he now indicated that he had private business to discuss, Hester suggested that Katherine should go and finish machining the new curtains, part of the preparations to make everything clean and pretty for Joanna.

Mr Bird, coming quickly to the reason for his out-of-time visit, explained that Mr Borden wanted to buy Miss Harper's land and he wanted to buy the farmhouse instead of renting it.

'Borden's place is doing very well.' Mr Bird wiped his tea wet lips on the back of his hand. 'It's the slope of his place and the movement of moisture,' he said. 'Funny how you can stand on the ridge out there and see a crop to one side of you and – on the other side – there's – well, there's nothing.' He shook his head. Hester knew what he meant. She had seen this for herself.

Mr Bird went on to say that he thought it would be a good thing if Miss Harper decided to sell. 'Price is good,' he said. 'At this stage you can insist on price – on your price. Borden wants to buy in here now. Might change his mind later. He's a good man,' Mr Bird paused and, without looking at Hester's stony face as if he needed to be unaware of her expression in order to be able to go on talking, he told her that he would help her, as always, with investments. 'You must look at it like this,' he said, his voice was steady not even persuasive. He was telling her plain facts he said. 'Borden has intentions to sub-divide. No, let me finish,' Mr Bird said quietly as Hester stiffened and was about to say, 'Never,' in a tone which he knew well. 'He can pay your price because he's going to get a lot more back. I happen to know. You know, yourself, the trend. It won't last but there it is, strike while the iron's hot, Miss Hester. Prices will drop, like lead they'll drop. Why? Drought.' The question and statement bounced between them. 'There's families,' he said, 'have walked off their farms in the past and there's families will be walking off them again. I'm not saying that you're in that position, Miss Hester, but you've the chance now to sail off and remember, your stubble's thin.'

Hester frowned till her dark eyebrows met. This trouble talk annoyed her. The idea of farmlets as they were called bored her.

'Once you've sold,' Mr Bird seemed to know her thought, 'what happens to the place is not your concern, you'll have no more say in the dealings, you'll quit but you'll have your own affairs to see to. Your money. Your slopes,' Mr Bird seemed ruthless. 'Your slopes,' he repeated, 'don't seem to conserve moisture as they once did. We're not doing as well as we should,' he added. He waited but as Hester made no reply he said, 'I'm an old man now, Miss Hester, I've nothing else to say. I'll not be able to help you forever. We, none of us, get any younger. There is just this too,' he paused, almost as if he was too shy to speak. 'there's a change in you, Miss Hester, if I can say this. For a long time now the farm's not been number one in your order of things. To put it plain, it's not a business any more.' He paused and then went on, 'And Borden, Mr Borden has asked me to make an offer on his behalf. It's a good offer. He's willing for you, if you so wish it, to keep this dog leg and this house, yard and shed buildings and he'll never trouble you at this end except to plough the firebreaks both sides of the fencing. It's a fair offer and open for you to ask more – it's all down here.' He gave Hester a sheet of paper.

Hester, receiving the letter with the written offer and the named price, sat silent, her eyes trying to read the formal words. She felt a pounding in her head as if all the blood vessels she had were filling and about to burst.

'Well think quick if you will please, Miss Hester,' Mr Bird said. He lowered his voice, 'And if I might advise you to hold your tongue about it before everyone, including little Miss Whatsaname in there.' He jerked his head towards the whirring sound of the sewing machine. Hester could not think of anything acid enough to say so she said nothing, managing, without any difficulty, to look like an advertisement for vinegar. Mr Bird stood up.

'Thank you, Miss Hester, for my tea. It would be better,' he said, 'to accept before Borden puts his fistful some place else.' With a final reminder that her stubble could be thicker and that they could both be younger he left.

During the night Hester, sitting in the moonlit window while Katherine brushed her hair gently, forgave Mr Bird his insult about her stubble. Never, she thought while the hairbrush steadily pressed the long sweeps of her strong hair downwards, had her paddocks looked so beautiful. From where they sat they looked across fold after fold of silent silvered stubble. In the moonlight the land seemed to be lifted up, raised as if held in offering towards the moon and the stars. Every stalk seemed clear and separate as if made of precious metal.

'Perhaps,' Hester said dreamily, 'perhaps I had better go

to town tomorrow and sell and sign and do whatever has to be done. Perhaps,' she added, having told Katherine word for word Mr Bird's confidential conversation, 'if we had some ready cash instead of it all being tied up in the property we could do a bit of travelling. See Europe. I'd like to take you to the places where I went when I was a girl. Beautiful! I remember,' she continued as if to herself, 'the swan waitress.' She laughed. 'You'd like to go wouldn't you Kathy, wouldn't you? eh?'

'Oh Miss Harper, dear, you will know best what should be done,' Katherine said, making a prim little mouth as she spoke. She told Hester to turn her head, 'A bit more Miss Harper, dear, so as I can brush the other side. Your hair's beautiful, Miss Harper, dear,' she purred. At the convent, she went on to remind Miss Harper, they all had to have their hair cut off, 'real short. Oh it was terribly ugly, you can have no idea.' She brought into her voice an American accent from *Saturday Night Fever* revived for the fourth time at the west-end drive-in cinema. 'So short and ugly,' she mourned, 'you reely can have no idea. We were all perfect frights!' Hester, having heard this lamentation more times than she could count, had her reply ready.

'Well yours has grown very well over the years,' she repeated comfortably in a voice reserved for remarks like this. She took the hairbrush. 'Sit down, Kathy, in front of me, like this and I'll do yours now. It's very soft and pretty, your hair, very fine and pretty.' Gently she began to brush Katherine's pale hair. The idea of travelling appealed very much. Suddenly it seemed possible that they would skim through the week of Joanna's visit and then deposit the guest at the railway station, perhaps even a day early; there would be a great deal of planning and arranging to do. Hester as she saw Katherine's hair shine in the moonlight under the steady brush began to think of charming little hotels in the Swiss Alps, in Paris and in Vienna. Yes, she thought, money would make all this possible.

The transaction, the agreement, all the decisions and the drawing up of documents for the sale took several weeks.

Mr Borden, to celebrate and to make his new ownership known, announced that he was giving a party and it would be held at the hotel. As Rosalie Borden said, it was a combination party as several people in the agreement were taking up small parcels of land immediately and it was also a way for Miss Harper to say farewell to her land. Quite an occasion really when you thought about it as the property had been Harpers since kingdom come. The hotel, she said, was to be taken over entirely for the night as anyone who was anyone in the township and the surrounding districts was to be invited. A great many friends and acquaintances of the Bordens lived in the city and would be coming. Some of these people, looking towards a leisured life on the land, had put down large sums of money to secure a small corner of Mother Nature.

The preparations went forward quickly. All the women with any pretence at being dressmakers were busy making and remaking dresses. There was to be a buffet supper (with caterers), laid out in both dining rooms. Seafoods and snacks would be served in the bars. And, in the yard there was to be a three-piece band and a specially laid and chalked dance floor. There was talk too of a disc jockey, records and coloured flashing lights.

Katherine was unable to sleep or to eat because of the excitement and the pleasure of anticipation. She talked of Joanna more and more. The letter still lay on the dresser.

'You know, Miss Harper, dear, Joanna's favourite song?'

'No I'm afraid I don't,' Hester counted the stitches in her knitting.

'Guess, Miss Harper, guess!'

'Oh no Kathy, I couldn't possibly.' Hester lost count and started again.

'Well,' Katherine said, It's one we might have at the dance. It's *Daddy don't you walk so fast,* it's not a new one now but I'm thinking of way back. Joanna was always singing it. She used to say she thought she could remember her father, his legs in a crowd of legs , trying to get away from her. She tried to go after him and kept seeing his legs through all the other legs and when she did get through, it wasn't him at all but another man who didn't want her. He was someone else's dad and he didn't want her. *Daddy don't you walk so fast. Daddy don't you walk so fast,'* Katherine sang in her American accent. It was a plaintive song and the words and the meaning touched Hester.

Accustomed to self examination and acts of contrition, Hester suffered more and felt that she ought to await Joanna's arrival with optimism and affection. She wished every minute of the day that she could get away with Katherine to some safe and harmless place. This thought was ridiculous as her place on the edge of the property was quite without harm. She had always felt perfectly safe once on the property as though nothing could touch her there. She told herself several times that she should not allow fear to enter her life like this.

'If only Joanna could be here sooner,' Katherine started the next morning with her chatter. She wished, she said, for Joanna to come at once. 'And then we could have twin matching dresses,' she said. 'Matching styles,' she added, 'but different colours, Miss Harper, dear. Joanna and me don't wear the same colours. Her hair is ever so much lighter than mine. She's real blonde! Ash blonde.'

Hester ignored the 'real' and corrected Katherine. 'Joanna and I,' she said, patience deserting her, 'Joanna and I.' She almost shouted the pedantic phrase. How could Katherine, after all this time, continue to make these mistakes.

'Oh no, Miss Harper, dear, it's me and Joanna I'm talking about. I wasn't suggesting for one minute that you should wear our styles. I mean, country and western wouldn't be yew? It wouldn't be right on yew, reelly it wouldn't.'

'Oh, never mind!' Hester snapped.

In spite of the smoothness of the sale and the feeling of relief and security at having money invested and money to spend she felt depressed. Mr Bird thought she would inevitably regret keeping so much money for spending. He was annoyed and tried not to show it.

'It's not the way, to live on your capital,' he said on his next visit and as if it came to him suddenly that Miss Harper was now no longer the land owner, he suddenly said quite rudely, 'If you go on the way you have been these last few years you'll be in the poor house.' He even shook a gnarled finger at her and she knew that he was refraining from making a coarse remark.

'Rubbish Mr Bird,' she said, 'there's no such thing nowadays as the poor house as you call it, and please, as before, mind your own business. I do not wish for advice. I am quite agreeable as I have always for you to continue to be an agent for me for certain investment but you will act on my instructions. Please remember this.'

'Very well, Miss Hester, if that's the way you want it,' Mr Bird said, and looking at the ground, he said, as if unable to resist the words of more advice, 'I do not think it right or wise, Miss Hester that you keep cash the way you do in the house. In your father's time it was different. You're asking to be robbed.'

'Nonsense Mr Bird, no one even knows the house is here.' Hester twitched her sleeves on the shoulders, first one and then the other, looking at each in turn.

'Times are different Miss Hester,' Mr Bird persisted. 'All kinds of people get to all kinds of places now. You could get a visitor, an unwelcome one, not invited, down that track any day.'

Hester, purposely misunderstanding, said, 'Nonsense I've been here for years and no one except yourself and, a few times, Mr Borden, has come to the cottage.' In the back of her mind though she was nervous and worried. She knew that was why she was being rude to Mr Bird. She seemed to see Joanna, the unknown threat; perhaps the vulgar creature would come in her own car, a panel van. Hester could see it, a white neglected panel van, dented and rusted with the remains of a picture, probably mountains, stencilled on one side. Joanna would arrive in her own cloud of dust. She would make her own skid marks, wiping out Miss Harper's at the sudden bend where the track turned by some rocks. The rocks marked the way in to the hidden yard. Unless a turn was made at the rocks a visitor would be likely to go on and miss the cottage altogether. The track itself disappeared into an old firebreak now overgrown with scrub and merging with a dried-out creek bed, an old water course which never ran with water. Hester thought there were salt lakes further on. Eerie places she said to Katherine once. They never went to investigate.

'You know perfectly well that no one ever comes here, we couldn't be more isolated,' she added conscious of a slight tremble in her voice.

Mr Bird, inclining his grey head, looked away for a moment and, undaunted, looked up at Hester again. 'There's people,' he said, 'as sometimes forget who their benefactors are.'

Miss Harper squinted down her long nose and made quick dismissing movements with her hands.

'I was going to say you should lock up your doors of a night and in the day time too when you go into town.' Mr Bird, ignoring her impatience, persisted. 'In town they all lock up now and they don't leave keys in cars, nor toys out overnight.'

Miss Harper remembered the little gardens on the edge of the township often scattered with broken toy scooters, shabby dolls' prams and bicycles. She snorted at the memory of this strewn poverty. It was just so much rubbish, people were welcome to take care of it if they wished.

'People have their treasures,' Mr Bird, as if knowing her thought, reminded her. 'And, if you'll forgive me saying this, there's some – not all but some who do forget who their benefactors are and it might in your case, only might I'm saying, be a case of shutting the stable door after the horse has bolted. Only in the circumstances I'm referring to the thing, and it's not a horse, the thing you might be needing to watch is already in the . . .'

Miss Harper interrupted Mr Bird by shrugging her thin shoulders almost up to her ears and turning her back on him.

The day of Borden's celebration came nearer. Hester wished that they need not go. Her own choice would have been to stay quietly at home. But Katherine, looking forward eagerly, was marking off the days on the kitchen calendar first to Mr Borden's party and then to the arrival of Joanna a few weeks later.

As the days went by Hester, who was planning extensive travelling in Europe and sending off for brochures, realized that she had promised Katherine things she did not feel equal to. She had the rolls of notes, a great deal of money she had insisted on keeping free from what she thought of as a burial in investment, Mr Bird having chosen and suggested which shares should be purchased for the highest and safest returns for her.

The thought of travelling frightened Hester. She was not used now to crowds of people. She knew from her childhood experience of travelling with Fräulein Hilde that people would be thronged, crushing against each other, in airports and on railway stations and even on pavements. Unused to traffic she would find crossing streets fearful. She knew she was afraid of being ill and feeling old and unable to manage in a strange hotel room. Though she had once been fluent in French and German she doubted that she would be able to understand either language if spoken by several people at once. And she knew how hard it was to compose a reply or a request in foreign words just when either were needed.

'*Trottel du Blöder! Aber Liebchen* say again *Ich möchte.* Make your mouth *Ö-so-Ich-möchte* . . . I wish . . . 'Hilde, Fräulein Herzfeld, patient and sweet voiced, urging her to pronounce words and phrases. Hester smiled remembering some little wrought-iron tables and a fair-haired waitress, like a swan, pushing her high bosom between the customers taking orders and moving off slowly, swan like, to fetch coffee and cakes. Hilde always made Hester order and the swan-waitress paused attentively before turning away once more, graceful in spite of being so large, to pause at the next table to gently bend her neck to smile and to listen and to write down on the clean little pad the names of the cakes. It was not possible to know, only to imagine, the swan-waitress sitting down at one of the white painted tables when all the customers had gone and, all alone, bending over a little mountain of cream-filled pastries.

On the day of the Borden's party Hester, straight after their early breakfast, listened to Mozart. She knew from listening alone that while she listened her mouth took on a different shape, the lips drawn together and pursed. Once, seeing her music-listening mouth in the rear mirror, while she was driving home with a string quartet in the cassette player she understood the possibility that her whole body was, during the music, different. Without meaning to she knew that it was not only her lips; it was all the seriousness and tenderness which entered and set the bones of her jaw and changed the movement of her eyebrows and the tilt of her head. The first time, the first time while driving home, she had been taken by surprise and mostly now she did not think of it.

This morning, removing herself from the preparations while Katherine was flying through the dishes and the poultry, she sat with the Mozart. For no special reason she remembered the four string quartets she had been to during the time at school. She remembered the dusty wooden platform, the stiff curtains looped back and the arrangement of potted palms and other green things in tubs on either side of the stage. The girls in their navy-blue Sunday dresses sat together in rows set aside for them. More important than these surroundings were the four performers themselves, the musicians, seated in quite an ordinary way on ordinary wooden chairs. It seemed as if they played in turn, one after the other, the first cautious notes gradually increasing in volume as each instrument invaded. They played towards each other leaning forward as if to make an emphasis and then pausing and leaning back allowing the phrases of music to follow one another and, in turn to meet and join, to climb and cascade.

It was the slight movements which the players made towards each other which touched Hester deeply then and which she remembered now. She remembered too the deep concentration which was evident in the sensitive movement of the muscles of their faces, particularly round the mouth. It was this which gave each player an expression of serious devotion. There was too the almost imperceptible inclining of the head and the drooping of the wrist and the slender white hand, the back of the hand displayed in such a vulnerable way towards the audience. These things would still be the same, she thought, if they were travelling and able to go to concerts in Europe.

'It's like going to the doctor's,' Katherine, glowing from the shower, partly covered in an expensive towel, interrupted Hester's quartet. 'All clean from the skin out,' she called, her voice resounding with excitement.

Hester showed her teeth in a reluctant and twisted smile and went to her room to dress.

'Who knows,' Katherine called, 'we might meet someone real nice. A real nice guy might be there. P'haps I'll meet Mr Right! Groovy eh? Mint eh?'

'Yes,' Hester said, selecting her clothes without pleasure. It crossed her mind all too often, though she tried not to let it, that she might have to give up Katherine.

'Perhaps today, tonight I should say, I'm going to meet my better half!' Katherine said in the doorway of Hester's room. 'How do I look Miss Harper, dear?' She skipped into the room. Hester who was saying 'never' inside her head turned round.

Katherine's dress was made from a very light material,

pale yellow, the palest yellow Miss Harper, dear, she had said when choosing the stuff. It had a ribbon embroidered with cornflowers at the waist and, for her hair, there was another similar little band. The blue embroidery matched her eyes. It had taken several evenings to make these decorations. Hester, regretting that she had to share Katherine's appearance with other people, pulled a dress from the wardrobe. She had decided to wear black as usual, a rusty black because the dress, though well made with hand-sewn covered buttons, was not new. The black exaggerated the pallor of her face. She put on too a woven jacket of natural wool. It was the only soft thing she ever allowed herself.

Katherine brushed and combed Hester's hair remarking that the streaks of grey at the temples were most attractive. 'The belle of the ball,' she said in one of her film-star accents. 'You're shivering Miss Harper, dear,' Katherine continued as they stood side by side to admire themselves in the handsome mirrors.

'Only a goose walking on my grave,' Hester said, suddenly glad, as an old person might be, of the woven jacket. It was of pure wool, spun and woven and sewn by them both. It was soft and light and warm and, as they both appreciated while gazing at themselves, looked well on the good quality, if ancient, black.

Mr Bird met them as they were picking their way across the rough ground at the back of the hotel.

'Borden could have had his affair up at the house,' Mr Bird said, 'would have had a different tone to it altogether . . .'

'I suppose he could,' Hester interrupted him in a cold voice. She was trying not to look at the hotel with the distaste she felt. She forced herself to smile.

'It's because of the dancing,' Katherine said quickly, seeing that Mr Bird had given her a wished for look of approval.

'Oh yes, the dancing. I was forgetting.' Mr Bird offered Hester his arm at the steps leading in to the verandah.

'Oh look! Miss Harper, dear,' Katherine exclaimed, 'there's the group, the band, real, it's all for real!'

Hester found herself immediately among people with whom she was not acquainted. This was something which, in earlier years, she had not been used to. The isolation of the last few years had been greater than she imagined. Perhaps she had not bothered to consider it. She realized without any effort on her part that these well-dressed, self-assured young couples – for they all were very self assured and they all were couples – were friends, naturally, of the new owners. They had come great distances to celebrate Borden's successful purchase. Hester thought of the airing of all the spare rooms at the farm house. She thought of her once well-cared-for stacks of blankets, the ends stitched and ribboned by herself. Though the deal had taken considerable time Harper's good reputation was, all at once, overnight it seemed, Borden's. A dull echo resounded in her head, not a headache exactly but a threat of one perhaps; the echo throbbed; Miss Harper's grand champion ewe, Miss Harper's prize-winning ram and Miss Harper's harvest. Harper's Place had become Borden's Place, the property of Mr Borden and his wife, Rosalie. Mr Borden said, she remembered, that he might keep the name Harpers Place. Hester knew that a place name came from what it, the place, was known by. She knew at once the place would be called Bordens. In her mind she saw the old house at dusk, closed up and secretive as she had seen it often, raised high on the slope facing west. She wished she had not come.

She stood gaunt and odd, pausing partly on her stick but mostly on Mr Bird's frail arm. She had not noticed before how thin he was now. It seemed impossible for her to feel that she was one of the guests in the crowded room. She could not recollect ever having felt quite like this. Mr Bird, seeing someone he knew, introduced her. The younger woman, scarcely looking, said, 'Pleased to meet you I'm sure,' in a cheerful voice and, reaching forward to clutch another guest by the arm, entered into an exciting conversation immediately, unavoidably turning a youthful chubby shoulder towards Miss Harper.

Both the Bordens hurried forward to greet Hester, Rosalie Borden telling Katherine that the dancing was about to start and couldn't she hear the drummer, a perfect pest he was and had she seen the disc jockey, 'So good looking my dear, you'll rave about him. Sure!'

'Oh Mrs Borden,' Katherine said, 'it's all beautiful, all the decorations and the lovely clothes. Do you like Miss Harper's dress?' she rushed on, 'It's not new but we made it from a Vogue pattern, didn't we Miss Harper, dear. It had to be done in eighty steps, my, it was an exercise!' Every night Miss Harper said, "this is an exercise." The lapels are feathered, Mrs Borden, and we made welted pockets and see the button cuffs,' she held up Hester's hand – now free from Mr Bird's arm. 'When the lapels are turned back,' Katherine continued, 'the feathering is underneath, and can you imagine covering a million tiny buttons!'

'A work of art, I'm sure Kathy,' Mrs Borden said laughing and glancing with tucked-in chin approval down her own simple maternity smock. 'Now just you go and see, Kathy, the dancers. You will be dancing yourself in a minute.' Mrs Borden turned to Hester. 'That girl is so old fashioned!' she continued. 'She's out of this world, quite delightful!' She shook her head as if doubting her own words and laughed again. Comfortable and rich Mr Borden, with the firm grip of the large landowner, shook hands with Hester.

Hester continued to wish that she had not come. Mrs Borden sighed with her lips drawn back over her polished teeth and pointed to the sofa.

'Let's be comfortable,' she said. 'Mr Borden will bring us drinks, won't you darl?'

'No need hon,' Mr Borden said as a pert waitress approached with a tray laden with brimming glasses.

'Ooo! I'm dying for a beer. Beer for you Miss Harper?' Rosalie Borden asked, her hand, sheathed in a cream glove, reaching to the tray.

'No thank you,' Hester replied more coldly than she intended.

'Ah! I remember, it's mozzle for you,' Mrs Borden said, 'I remember you like the sweet wines. Quite a lot of people do,' she added kindly. 'Ah! here's Mr Bird, he's bringing a glass for you. He knows what you drink. I must say I like a sweet wine myself even though the hoy polloy, or whatever, express a preference for dry.' Rosalie Borden's flat voice went on. It seemed to Hester that whatever Mrs Borden said it would turn out to be either spiteful or incredibly dull.

Mr Borden, seeing his chance, escaped to a group of prosperous looking men who were grouped like cattle at the far end of the room. Looking across at him Hester could not help thinking of the fleshy shoulders of the mating bulls. Mr Borden gave the impression of setting about the male task of servicing frequently and thoroughly with a view to enriching his property with a number of sons. The Bordens already had six little boys being raised to reward the farm in the way that well-bred cattle reward. Rearing cattle and children, Hester knew, was a part of farming. Her maidenly mind was quite capable of vividly imagining Mr Borden in performance. She did not blush at her own thoughts as Mrs Borden would have done if she had known exactly what was in the mind of her elderly guest who knew too that there was a certain obligation on the part of the new landowner's wife to take care of her during the horrible evening.

Hester in the presence of so many clean couples, for they all did look so well washed and ironed, wondered at their cleanliness in relation to their own cowshed activities. These would not even show in the pastel chenille bedrooms. It was a subject for endless speculation of a private sort and perhaps was a way of preventing the awful feeling which crept ever nearer of being now entirely without consequence. No one would ever make conversation with her again in order to catch a hint of wisdom about what to buy and what to avoid at the next sale.

Every now and then Hester was aware, during their conversation, of Mrs Borden's eyes darting here and there as she recognized someone she knew. It seemed that many of the women, Rosalie Borden included, were wearing hats. These hats of brilliant green or red and black felt were like the hats fairytale huntsmen wore. The hats had something in common, a high rounded crown and a wide curling brim which dipped down over the nose leaving one predatory eye always on the look out. The splendid teeth exposed in smiles beneath these huntsmen's hats enhanced the keen hungry look which seemed to predominate.

Hester thought she had a headache coming on. Her lame leg ached and she was not without uncharitable thoughts towards Joanna's visit. There were qualities in Katherine which could break out unpleasantly, she felt, well unpleasantly as far as she herself was concerned if Katherine was to be in the wrong company. The nearby pounding of the music made her feel dizzy. In her truthful way she told herself that she was dreading Joanna's visit and that she felt old and that she was no longer a respected landowner. The sharp little smile she often gave when she was thinking twisted her lips as she, with even more honesty, told herself that her lack of interest, which amounted to neglect, towards the property as she became more caught up with her life with Katherine was enough to cause her to lose respect among the farmers she knew. Her loss, brought on by her own actions, was serious, she admitted this. In her hand the thick tumbler of insipid white wine seemed intensely cold. It made her hand ache. The quantity of wine was, as if from a profound and natural ignorance, too great. She had been given as much wine as Rosalie had beer.

'Cheer ho!' Rosalie Borden daintily with pursed bright lips syphoned some foam from the top of her drink. 'Ah!' she said, 'it's the first biting swallow that does it. That wonderful first gulp!'

'I suppose it is,' Hester said in a flat voice. She had never depended on anyone, or so she thought. She hoped, deeply, that Rosalie Borden, even though she did not care for her at all, would not desert her.

'Have another drink,' she suggested to Rosalie in a voice straining to be cordial but which was pathetic and hopeful. Seeing the glass drained in a most professional and even masculine way, she tried to open her handbag.

'Heavens no!' Rosalie said, 'thank you very much.' She put her hand over the clasp of Hester's bag. 'Ah! oops! I think I'm going to burp,' she laughed. 'Mr Borden would kill me if he saw me drink like that but I really was dry and junior,' here she patted her maternal fullness, 'craves beer, you'd never believe! If I have another drop I'll be on my ear.' She laughed again and leaning towards Hester she was suddenly serious. 'I expect,' she said, 'that you feel quite bereaved.'

'Why, yes,' Hester was surprised into admission and at once regretted her indiscretion. It had always been her way to be aloof and withdrawn so that she, in a position of authority with a good head for crops and wool, was beyond gossip and criticism. She had with two words, she knew, made herself available for unlimited speculation.

'You know, there's something I have been wanting to say to you for some time,' Mrs Borden, still serious, dropped her voice. 'I hope you will understand . . .'

'Yes?' Hester moved uneasily on the uncomfortable sofa. She leaned forward, inclining her head with a stiff movement. In the tremendous noise it was hard to hear. 'Well yes,' Mrs Borden echoed Miss Harper's way of speaking, 'we don't, that is Mr Borden and I don't think, that is, we think that it is not right to keep Katherine, a young woman like Katherine shut away. I mean, she must think of men, a man? Sometimes?' The hat brim dipped forward deeply and then came up again and Hester had Rosalie Borden's bright inquisitive eyes directly opposite her own. 'You must realize,' her voice changed to a teasing note, 'that not every woman wishes to remain single.' The two women glanced quickly, Hester's glance following Mrs Borden's at the room full of couples and intending couples. As Hester made no reply Mrs Borden rushed on. 'I don't want to seem interfering,' she said, 'but it does seem that Katherine is intelligent. She could be a teacher, primary of course, or had you thought of nursing as a career?' She paused and then continued, 'Or if not a career, she must surely be thinking of wedding bells? This might sound old fashioned,' Mrs Borden laughed, 'but then she is what I call an old-fashioned girl. She is very pretty in a pale sort of way, she should be ...' Mrs Borden, seeing the cold tight expression on Hester's face, changed the subject. 'Perhaps,' she said, 'we should go and watch the dancing. Shall we?'

'Oh yes, of course,' Hester, wishing to be independent of Rosalie Borden's plump kindly arm, struggled to her feet. 'I must watch the dancing,' she said with a grudging little smile as if offering a kindness when she knew privately that it gave her infinite secret pleasure to watch Kathy abandon herself to her own energy. Whenever she watched Kathy dancing, Hester, though outwardly showing no signs, moved in a wonderful freedom within herself. Her tiniest, most obscure muscles all took part. Unseen, her heart beat faster. She breathed more rapidly. In the privacy beneath her strict clothing she knew she was capable of an inner excitement which belonged only to her. It was a solitary experience but she did not mind this, being simply grateful for it. The music, the beat and the rhythm of the dancing filled her with a glow of satisfaction and a realization of deep happiness. She felt as if she had been singing and dancing, moving in time with the music and with other people. She felt as if her hair was loose and as if her clothes were bright and light and as if they moved too, easily with her own rhythm. She felt free of bitterness, jealousy and longing. She was free from anxiety; who minded now, at this moment, about drought or about floods. She forgot she was lame and had always to depend upon a stick.'

'I don't suppose you care for all this modern stuff.' Mrs Borden's voice, close to Hester, broke in upon the sweetest consolation.

'I don't dislike it,' Hester said.

Their voices were lost in the beat of the music.

'You should bring Katherine to the dances in town,' Mrs Borden bellowed with the drums. 'Would make a late night for you,' she shouted, 'but you could always sleep in, especially now, you being a lady of leisure.' Liking the phrase she repeated it, 'A lady of leisure.'

Hester, not attempting a reply, nodded again. A lady of leisure living on a dog leg, she reflected, the owner of a special deed drawn up by lawyers for Mr Borden and herself. Mr Borden was not a bad young man, quite fair minded, Hester admitted to herself, she was pleased with the agreement. You couldn't eat land, she knew this, neither could you spend it. At the end of his life, even while he was dying, her father worried endlessly about the property. At least, Hester thought, she would not end her days, thank you very much, muttering curses because the rain clouds were thin. If there was a sour side to the pleasure of the agreement it must be accepted. She had not considered earlier how she would feel when the land spreading out towards the horizon was no longer hers. She had not bargained either with the thought that the wife of the new owner would start at once telling her what she ought to do. She tried to concentrate on the dancing.

Katherine with her head thrust forward and down was moving jerkily, like a wooden doll, towards them, her eyes were empty of expression and her mouth was slightly open. She shook her shoulders and let her arms hang by her sides. She let the shoulder-shake slide to her hips. She moved to the right and to the left advancing steadily towards Hester and Mrs Borden. When the music stopped abruptly the dancers, as if frozen, stood still. Katherine had one leg forward and one back and both arms were raised and her head was lifted so that her hair was thrown back. Hester saw, with fondness, the beads of moisture on her upper lip. The music started again and the dancers, as if they had never stopped, went on dancing.

Hester sat with a little smile in the corners of her mouth. Katherine was walking or rather prancing with a springing step the length of the dance floor and back. She turned her head and moved her shoulders as her favourite John Travolta moved his head and shoulders. Back and forth she stepped lightly and, when the music changed, she began again to dance. Hester knew that this was what Kathy always longed for.

'Kathy's enjoying herself,' Mrs Borden said. 'It's a pretty dress, Miss Harper, that Kathy's got. I guess you made it together. But it's too nave. Pardon me for saying so but the dress is too nave. I guess it's the Peter Pan collar . . .'

'I'm sorry?' Hester had not heard. 'What did you say?'

'I said,' Mrs Borden said, 'and pardon me for having the courage of my new position,' she laughed with considerable noise, 'pardon me for saying this,' she said, 'that dress, Kathy's not her age in it. It's too nave, but.'

'Oh, I see, naïve,' Hester understood. She was deeply hurt by the remark, painfully as if Kathy might have heard it too and been wounded. 'It depends on what you want,' she said, feeling that she must answer but not able to say what she really would have liked to say.

People, it seemed to Hester as she followed Mrs Borden through the crowd to the supper room, did not pause to greet her as they once would have done. And no one moved aside to make way for her to pass. She tried to hurry, trying to squeeze between people in order not to lose sight of her hostess. Though she did not care at all for Mrs Borden she was anxious not to be alone. She kept her eyes on the florid pregnant figure ahead. She was now, she understood, fully on the same footing as the common townspeople.

'How does it feel?' Mr Bird asked her as he came towards her carrying an oval plate of chips and fried fish unsuitably decorated with lettuce. Some leaves fell off as Mr Bird came nearer. He steadied the pile of thick bread and butter with a rough thick finger. 'How does it feel,' he repeated the words when he was close enough, 'to have all that solid cash behind you eh? Better than dry paddocks eh?'

'Oh, so so,' Hester replied unwilling to reveal that his speaking of the money like this comforted her. Mr Bird, as he had done before, though she would never thank him for it, was bringing her comfort. Suddenly she remembered that during both her years at boarding school Mr Bird had sent her birthday cards. He had simply added his initial and his surname to the message inside the cards. Hester, not having many letters and certainly none from men, made much of the cards and the sender of them to the girls at school . . .

'Here,' he said, 'take it, I've brought it for you. There's a place over there, make for that table there and we'll sit down a while.' Hester, with gratitude, did as she was told. She was hungry of course. They had had their small lunch very early and nothing since.

'Remember,' Mr Bird said, watching her eat, 'don't disclose your assets to anyone and don't take anyone into your confidence. Not about your money anyhow. And,' he added in a low voice, 'give up that red woollen bonnet!'

Hester smiled and sucked her greasy fingers. 'Perhaps,' she said, her old arrogance coming back. She would keep her money any way she wanted to. 'I'll think about it,' she said.

'As well as the investments you've got,' Mr Bird said, 'I've got something else for you. I'll bring the papers for you to sign. I really mean what I say about not having cash to that amount around the place – won't do you any good just to let it lie.'

'Thanks,' Hester said as coldly as she could through the white flesh of the fish. As she ate she felt more comfortable. She felt comfortable thinking of her money. There was considerable reassurance in having some, a large amount, in a place where she could peer at it as into a nest from time to time as often as she liked. Mr Bird fetched her a cup of tea. As she drank it a mellowness which accompanies tea when it is brought as an offering spread through her. Perhaps one day, not just now, she would remind Mr Bird of the birthday cards and thank him for them.

Hester needing to visit the Ladies Room made her way slowly through the crowd and, as she passed the open doors to the bar, she was greeted warmly by the men who had worked for her. She responded strangely grateful for an unexpected show of friendship. Emboldened by her apparent good humour one of the men made a remark which caused Hester to give one of her loud snorts of braying laughter. She steadied herself against the door post and several of the men joined in her laugh.

Immediately Mrs Borden was at Hester's side. 'Sssh!' she was hissing and rearing, clutching at Hester's arm. 'Mr Borden,' the hiss was vehement, 'Mr Borden is just addressing his guests. Keep your voice down. Do! If you can!' Anger flashed from the eyes under the huntsman's hat. In the look of anger Hester saw all too clearly a look of distaste amounting to hatred. Other people, she noticed, were still talking. She was not the only one, there was considerable noise everwhere except in the bar where the men were now looking on in silence. With a final glare Mrs Borden released Hester's arm and went back to her husband's speech forcing a smile which lifted her scarlet lips well off her teeth. Still smiling she took up a possessive position at his side. As Hester turned to move away as quickly as possible a camera flash startled her and she realized that in all probability her uneasy hurt face might well appear in the pictures of the celebrations in the local newspapers the next day.

Hester and Katherine did not speak much on the long drive home. At first it was a moonlight night, very dry and clear. The chill air carried the fragrance of the ploughed earth. Liking this but wishing for the sharp scent of rain on the paddocks Hester reflected, as she often did, that the nights in the wheat were either moonlit or quite black. She settled herself in the passenger seat and noticed that the moon was sliding into dark ribs of cloud. She shrugged and yawned.

Katherine, elated with the evening, had insisted on driving. 'Yew sit back and take a rest Miss Harper, dear,' she had tucked the small tartan rug over Hester's bony knees. 'If I'm to get my test next week,' her purring voice soothed, 'I'd better get in some practice hadn't I.' As Hester fumbled with the ignition key which she wore on the chain around her neck Katherine's neat quick fingers helped themselves. 'Make a good burglar wouldn't I,' she laughed as she slipped into the driver's seat.

The best part of the evening, Hester reflected was Kathy's dancing, the girl's energetic rhythmic movements. The yellow dress at times, in spite of Mrs Borden's attack, had been like a light flickering now here and now there. The misty quality of the material had been just right, Hester felt that Kathy's dress was in fact the prettiest one there. The music and the dancing were the pleasures of the evening. Also, she smiled to herself, it was sweet of Katherine to leave the dancing and come over the way she had, knowing Hester's weakness for sweet things.

'Miss Harper dear, I thought you'd like the sherry trifle.'

'Oh naughty Kathy, all that cream, what'll it do to my waist!' Together they had disposed of quite a large plateful Katherine having brought two spoons.

The road between black paddocks was flat and strange as though they had never travelled along it before. Swirls of white mist came towards them and sometimes when there was a dip in the road they were completely enshrouded in a light white endlessly winding garment. The surrounding countryside, Hester said, could seem desolate and frightening for anyone travelling especially if they had no home to go to. Katherine agreed, she for one would not want to drive the road at night alone. 'I'm glad we're together Miss Harper, dear,' she said.

Pleasantly lulled with thoughts of Katherine's happiness at the dance and with looking forward to her own warm bed Hester slept. She hardly noticed when they turned off the road on to the track.

It seemed, as she roused herself, that Kathy was driving too fast.

'Katherine! Not so fast,' she warned. 'Katherine! Not so

fast I said. Watch the track. You're going too fast, slow down. Katherine! For heaven's sake! Do be careful. You'll have us roll over if you drive like this. Please Kathy! Katherine! You'll lose your licence before ever you get it!'

Katherine did slow down. 'I guess I'm still excited Miss Harper, dear,' she said. 'I'm sorry if I scared yew.' She was carefully as American as possible. She went on to remind Miss Harper how exciting it was that Joanna would be with them in time for the fête and that she had a wonderful idea for the jam and pickle stall. 'Oh Miss Harper, dear,' she said, 'we could be right out of Shakespeare.' She paused. 'I could be Rosalind, I'd love to be Rosalind and Joanna could be Orlando. I'd so love to wear a doublet and hose. We could make the costumes. Mine would be a woodland green and for Orlando, Miss Harper, do you think purple and . . . oh it would be perfect and would be something quite fresh and new at the fête. Romantic! Miss Harper, dear, love interest! If Joanna and me could be married together. A double wedding. We could drive off like this to an all revealing honeymoon – like in a film! It must be nice to be married to the man of your dreams,' she said. For reply Hester gave one of her snorts to which there was no answer.

'Oh Miss Harper,' Katherine said after a short silence, 'could I make some baby clothes, for the stall? We could have a section at the side of the miscellaneous gifts next to the tea cosies and the knitted pochettes – you know, little dresses, baby dresses, I would so like to do some smocking. And, I know!, little bibs trimmed with lace . . . Please! I know they'd sell.'

'Babies eat their lace,' Hester said grimly. 'Keep your mind on the car,' she added.

Katherine pressed her foot harder on the accelerator. The sturdy truck seemed to leap forward on the ridged gravel.

'Kathy!' Hester's voice was tense. 'Kathy! we're nearly at the bend. Slow down! I can see the bend. Kathy!'

'Oh wasn't it a lovely party!' Katherine began, in her piping voice, to sing,

Dinga Donga Bella Yair Yair
Pussa inna wella Yair Yair Yair
Dinga Donga Bella Yair Yair Yair Yair Huh!

'Wow! Miss Harper! I sure enjoyed myself!'

'I'm glad of it Kathy,' Hester said, 'but for heaven's sake do slow down.

Pussa inna wella
Hoohah putta inna Yair yair yair
Dinga Donga Bella Yair yair . . .

'Oh don't keep singing that crazy song,' Hester was cross. 'I can't think how anyone would think a nursery rhyme could be a song for dancing – whatever that ridiculous dance was.'

'The pussycat freeze, Miss Harper, dear, it was the pussycat freeze, did you like it Miss Harper! eh?' She pressed her thumb on the horn. 'The break dance huh? eh?'

'Stop the car Katherine, I'll drive.'

'Wee wopp! Here we go! Oops caught the bushes. Blast! Shit! Oops. Sorry, Miss Harper. Hit that rock. Always get that rock,' she laughed in a shrill voice. 'Wish Joanna could've been here tonight. Wish you were here Joanna!'

'Look out! There's something on the track. Look out! Brake Katherine ! Brake. Oh look out! Oh God! The bend!' Hester's shriek stopped abruptly as something hit the car with a heavy dull thud. Katherine stopped the car, the engine was still running.

'I think we've hit a roo.' Hester, grabbing her stick, clambered with difficulty from the truck and limped to the front. 'It's not a roo,' she called in a low voice. 'Don't come out. Stay where you are!' She moved slowly round to Katherine's side. 'It's horrible,' she said, 'it's caught up on the bar. It's . . .'

'But there's never anyone on the track . . .'

'Be quiet Katherine! There may be someone else around.' Hester's voice was low and urgent. 'I'm trying to think what's the best thing to do. For God's sake, don't start to howl. We must keep as quiet as we can.'

'But there's never anyone on the track . . .'

'It seems there was this time. For heaven's sake don't howl!'

'Miss Harper! do you think he's been to our place?'

'How should I know. Now listen,' Hester leaned on the open window. 'Listen I want you to do exactly as I tell you. We haven't any choice Kathy. And we may not have much time. We must get out of here. As quick as we can.'

'Is he hurt bad?' Katherine began to sob.

'Stop that Miss! Stop it at once!' Hester raised her voice. Put off the lights – I want you to drive slow. Slow as you can, as quiet as you can. I'll be here alongside. We'll get in the yard back of the woolshed. When you're in the yard I want you to turn, slow – I don't want it to fall off. I'll keep near. The ground's rough. I don't know what's track and what's shadow. Now drive. Come on. Slow and careful. Come on!'

Hester, as she walked, heard the wind coming across the paddocks which were no longer hers. 'Kathy,' she said, 'we have to do this. Drive as close to the well as you can, straight at the well. Yes, I said the well. There's nothing wrong with the Toyota. We've got to get this off the bar. Just get as near, as close to the well as you can.'

The little cortège moved slowly forward towards the rhythmic rise and fall of the derelict well cover.

'For God's sake don't cry like that!' Hester had to hiss because she was afraid of the sound of her voice crossing the darkness. 'Save your breath and help me to break the tin a bit more.'

Katherine crouched in the shelter of the coping. Hester put her hands on her shoulders. 'Come along Kathy, help me, it's the only thing we can do.' She caressed Katherine gently. 'You'll catch cold there on the ground,' her pleading voice broke through the hissing.

Hester worked on alone. It was a desperate work. At last she considered the opening to be big enough. The well, about to receive the unexpected gift, was strangely silent. Cold air came steadily from the black depths. Katherine seemed to have disappeared into the rough black stone work. With tremendous effort Hester pulled and heaved to unhook the body. At last it sagged in a thick curve along the low wall of the well, on the place where they often sat, low, near the warm earth, in summer.

'I'll never sit here again,' Katherine's voice came out in a little whimper.

'Nonsense! of course you will,' Hester said sharply. She had a pain in her back. She was afraid too that the hole would not be large enough. She felt she was using all her strength and that it would not be enough. She made one final effort groaning aloud as she did so. The body disappeared, without protest, off the edge of the low wall scraping and breaking more off the rotting cover. There was no other sound at all. He did not even seem to hit the sides as he went down.

Hester stared into the widened black hole. The horror of what she was doing only came over her when it was done.

'A quick burial,' Hester was trembling. A sickening feeling of weakness enveloped her. She felt as if she would cry. Small darts of light like lightning flashed by her right eye. It was a symptom she had had before. There was no light really. She knew this but found herself peering about in the dark for the source. She had a pounding in her head and she had to steady herself on the coping of the well.

'But the car, it might show . . .' Katherine said in a whining little girl voice.

'There, there, Kathy,' Hester said in a low voice, 'it's all over. We'll look in the morning, that roo bar's as tough as they come, probably there'll be no mark and what if there's a dent of two? Who's to notice? But come on, we'll catch cold out here, both of us. Come on. I'll light the chips. What we need is a good hot tub to warm us up. Come along in Kathy.' Fumbling for her pocket she pulled out her handkerchief for the tears which would not stop.

Already long fingers of a pale honey-coloured light were creeping across the place where the endless black paddocks merged with the endless black sky. The sky was noticeably lighter as they entered the house together and closed the door.

Because of the disturbing experience Katherine got into bed with Hester, hers being the larger bed. Both declared they would be unable to sleep. But both must have dozed Hester realized when she, waking, heard the usual rattle and tapping of the well cover in the wind. Accustomed to these noises she turned over as carefully as she could. It was touching that Katherine, desiring safety and comfort, had asked to sleep beside her.

'Miss Harper! Miss Harper!' Hester heard Katherine as in a dream; 'Miss Harper!'

'What is it Kathy?' She must have been asleep again.

'I heard a noise Miss Harper. Listen! What's that noise? There it is again,' Katherine's whisper strained in the greyness.

'It's only the old well cover, dear, you should know that. I'll close the window.' Hester, leaning out of bed, pulled the small window shut. 'I expect it's looser now,' she said, 'and rattles more.'

'No, Miss Harper,' Katherine, half sitting up, whispered. 'No, not the wind, Miss Harper, another noise. It's someone, it's a person. Miss Harper, there's someone in the room.'

Both women, half sitting up, not moving and hardly breathing, listened. There was a noise, a faint noise of movement, strangely close to them. It suggested merely skin and bones, dry, rasping lightly on each other, eerie and haunting.

It is not possible, Hester reasoned, for two people to have the same nightmare. She struck a match and lit the lamp.

83 ☆

'There,' she said, 'it's this; it's only a moth, a big one.'

The moth fluttered and limped after hitting itself on the lamp glass. It settled for a few dizzy seconds on the edge of the embroidered cloth which covered the chest of drawers at Hester's side of the bed. 'It's only a poor moth, your intruder,' Hester, knowing her heart was pounding, laughed. She turned the lamp-wick down.

They lay back on their pillows once more. The dark room was filled with the reassuring fragrance of kerosene which slowly gave way to the sharp sweetness of over-ripe quinces. A box of them was on the top of the wardrobe. Hester, watching the little square window, saw the remains of the night sky change to the pale, washed-out light of the morning. She thought it would be a good idea to start making the quince preserves and jelly. Then she remembered the truck. After examining the truck she would start on the quinces. She and Katherine would cut them together. It was pleasant to look forward to the hot fragrance in the kitchen and ultimately, as she remembered them, to the little jars (she always used small pretty jars for quinces) of clear rosy jelly in rows on the kitchen table.

Miss Harper's jam-and-pickle shed was a well-known part of the town fête every year. Hester had carried on the tradition from her grandmother who always said that raising money to help those less fortunate than yourself was God's work. Hester, liking the idea of working for God occasionally, together with Katherine continued the effort and, always, their stall was one of the most popular. Lying in as comfortable position as she could Hester counted the specially made costumes. One year Katherine was a little Dutch girl, then a Japanese fisherman, another year, a Spanish dancer, the next, a Russian peasant, the next, and this time she wanted something from Shakespeare and, of course, Joanna . . . She tried to think of the shelves already laden with bottled tomatoes. The vision of the healthy jars was comforting. She heard Katherine's deep breathing as she slept soundly on her side of the bed. No one must ever know of the accident. Hester set her mouth in a firm line. If this thing, now called 'the accident' in her own mind, was ever known about everything they had would be disturbed and spoiled. She was determined that the whole thing was to be considered over and done with. She thought of the words she would use at breakfast time to impress this serious thought on Katherine once and for all time.

She turned over. She was restless. Her lame leg ached. Mrs Borden's remark about Katherine's dress was hurtful. Mrs Borden's voice came to her. She was keeping Katherine too young was she. But wasn't it just the youthfulness of the attractive girl, dressed up so sweetly, which brought everyone to the jams and pickles. Even the meanest men and women went away laden with jars. Hester turned over again and tried to recapture something safe and wholesome in the fragrance of the quinces.

'The kitchen.' Hester was roused once more. Katherine was sitting up in bed. 'The kitchen!' she seemed hardly able to whisper. 'Miss Harper, there's a noise in the kitchen. Listen.'

Hester raised herself on one stiff elbow. Both women listened. From indoors came the drip drop of the kitchen tap and from outside the familiar tap tapping of the well cover as it stirred above the new inhabitant.

'There's nothing there Kathy,' Hester said. The short sleep had made her feel heavy and her throat was dry. 'I'll have a look,' she said, 'I'll make us some tea.' Her head ached. She hoped she was not going to have one of her migraines. She hoped too, while the kettle rattled to the boil, that Katherine was not going to go all nervy. There were tonics, she thought, that could be bought, something to steady the nerves. She tried to think of names she had seen on advertisements but could only remember pictures of distressed faces and hands holding troubled heads. Katherine coming quietly on bare feet into the kitchen made her jump. 'Nearly out of my skin! Kathy, you gave me a fright.' She laughed forgetting for a moment all that was so heavy on her mind. 'I've made the tea, we'll take it back to bed and . . .'

'Miss Harper!' Katherine screamed, bringing both hands up to her mouth as if to try to stop the scream. 'Miss Harper! Look! There – behind –' she pointed to the floor beyond Hester's trailing shawl.

Hester turned to look and saw on the tiles of the floor the red woollen hat. There was nothing unreasonable about the red hat. Hester said so. 'It's only the hat Kathy,' she said with a steady quietness in her voice. 'I must have knocked it off the dresser. You put it back, dear, it's easier for you to bend down and . . .'

'Miss Harper!' Katherine's next scream was even more piercing, 'there's nothing in it, it's empty.' She held out the hat letting it dangle, without life, from her thin fingers. Hester grabbed it and turned it inside out. With a quick nervous movement she looked along the shelves of the dresser pushing the plates aside. She looked on the floor, under the table, she moved the chairs, scraping them in her agitation. She pulled open the cupboards. She looked at her own empty helpless hands. 'He must have been in the house.' Disgust made her choke. The round tea tray on the edge of the table suddenly seemed shabby and pathetic. Hester cried at the sight of it. 'Oh,' she moaned as if to her-self, 'what have I done. What have I done.'

'He,' Katherine paused, the word seemed to make her self-conscious. Hester glanced at her sharply. 'He,' Katherine said again, stammering, 'he must have had the money on him when . . .' again she brought both hands up to her mouth as if to hold in the words.

'Yes – yes – of course I realize that.' Hester's voice was ugly and loud, its loudness made them both silent. 'We can't tell anyone Katherine,' she said, 'we must not tell anyone, not one single person must know.' She turned the hat inside out. She twisted it over and over again as if the movement in some magic way could bring back the rolls of notes. Something would have to be done as quickly as possible. 'We can't ask anyone, Katherine,' Hester said. Even if she still had reliable men working for her it would not have been possible to ask one of them to climb down to retrieve the money. The idea was ludicrous. She gave a short bark of laughter. 'The money must be got back straight away,' she said, spacing the words out for emphasis. 'Katherine-I-do-not-wish-for-hysteria-of-any-sort. Listen to me!' She advanced towards Katherine steadying herself on one of the high-backed chairs. 'You will have to go down the well and get the money.' They stood for a moment, in silence, looking at one another. Hester moved forward a step. 'Kathy,' she said in a cajoling tone, 'it will not be at all difficult. I'll get a rope, a good one, today. I'll go to town. Tonight, when it's dark we'll get our money back.'

'It's your money, not mine,'Katherine said, 'and I'm not going down there. I won't go. I can't! It's too horrible. I can't ... I ...'

'Katherine!' Hester said, 'do you want us to starve?'

'That's not all the money you've got, Miss Harper.'

'That's beside the point. It happens to be our ready money, we need it right away.'

'Not ours, it's yours. Yours! I didn't put it down there.'

'Katherine, you must surely understand, it's too much to simply lose like that. You will do as I say and go . . .'

'I won't! He's dead. I'd have to touch a dead man. I might have to look for the money on him, I'd have to touch him,' Katherine began to cry. 'I'm going to be sick. Miss Harper, he might have it next to his body, next to his skin, I couldn't do it.'

'Yes I know he's dead, Katherine,' Hester's voice was low and grim, 'and I'll remind you who killed him. Just remember who it was who killed him. Now, you stay here today while I go into town for a proper rope. If we don't do this thing as soon as possible I don't need to tell you it will be worse to do later. The rope we have is too old. We can't risk it.'

'But Miss Harper, it was an accident. I didn't run over him on purpose. You know that.' Katherine clasped her thin fingers together. 'Miss Harper, what if there's something else down there, it's enough that He's there. I can't, Miss

Harper, I can't do it. I won't,' her voice rose and stayed on a hysterical note. She sank down on to the other chair.

'Katherine be quiet!' Hester was like a monument in the small kitchen. I'll have to remind you,' she said, 'think will you, who killed him? Eh? Who? Also, I will ask you this. Do you want to go back to the Orphanage? Do you?'

'The Home? Miss Harper?' Katherine stared up at Hester. 'Miss Harper, I couldn't go back there. Miss Harper, I couldn't,' her voice was thin, almost a whisper, 'I'm too old, Miss Harper, I couldn't go back now. They don't have grown-up people there, only girls. I'm not a girl any more Miss Harper.' She stood up. 'You can't send me back there, Miss Harper, they wouldn't have me.'

Hester, keeping her lips together said, 'The orphanage or prison.' Again there was a silence during which they stared at each other as if lost in a strange place. Katherine was no longer crying. 'Now pull yourself together,' Hester said, 'we must get dressed and have our breakfast. I'll make some fresh tea. Come along.' She put an arm out towards Katherine, 'We'll manage, we have to. I'll be away all day, and you must go to bed. You need a good sleep.' Hester longed to take back her words and show fondness. She kept her voice low and steady and did not reveal her feelings.

'Oh Miss Harper, dear, please don't go, don't leave me all alone here all day.' Katherine seemed to throw herself at Hester's stern body.

'There, there,' Hester took her in her arms but quickly held her stiffly away at arm's length. 'We must be sensible and calm,' she said, almost losing her balance. She wanted to say how she would go down the well herself but she was so hampered by the useless leg. She was not in the habit of mentioning the leg and did not know how to say what she would have liked to say. Instead she repeated in a gruff voice the same words, 'There, there,' knowing that she must not show any weakening in her resolution. She would, she thought, remind Katherine time after time that no one must ever be told, not even a hint, that if there were marks or dents on the truck they had been made by stones flying up from the track. She would remind Katherine of the convent. There would be no harm in suggesting discipline. All the time she was thinking of the effort needed to make a show of preparing a meal and eating it. She knew she must make the effort.

Mr Bird's early-morning arrival was preceded by flocks of screeching cockatoos. These marauding pirates, on their way to other places, swooped and circled in their noisy ragged flight. They seemed to suggest the encompassing of spaciousness and freedom and an enjoyment of something known only to themselves. They seemed entirely without responsibility. Hester, seeing, in the distance, the advancing cloud of dust in which Mr Bird was making steady progress across Borden's dry paddocks, seized a basin and, when he clambered down from his small truck, she crossed the yard throwing grain to the poultry and hurrying towards him. He, because of this, stayed on the other side of the wire fence. After an exchange of comments on the celebration of the night before Mr Bird came straight to the point.

'I've the papers on me.' he said. 'You can invest more than half of what you've kept in the house. I've got everything we need, all you've got to do is sign.' He patted his breast pocket. 'If you'll sign,' he said, 'I'll come in for your signature and a quick look at the teapot, eh? I meant what I said last night, Miss Hester, I'm getting old and I'd like to see you safe. It's not right to live off any of your capital. You know that. I don't need to explain to you . . .'

'Mr Bird,' Hester interrupted him, 'I'll trouble you not to push down on the top wires like that. I could never stand seeing a fence take a man's weight. I should have thought that you of all people, you wouldn't. . .'

'No harm meant, Miss Hester. I came across this way, rough though it is, to be quicker,' he paused. 'Where's young Katherine then?' He shaded his eyes to look across the busy yard. Still in her bed is she? After all that dancing?

Miss Hester,' he lowered his quiet voice, 'Miss Hester, I'd like us to settle this in private.'

'There's no need,' Hester replied quickly. 'I've invested all I mean to, thank you. I thought I'd made this perfectly plain. There's no more to say about it.'

Mr Bird seemed to understand. Slowly he handled the papers he had started to bring out of his pocket. He began to fold them and put them back. 'Well, if that's the story,' he said, 'but I can tell you a mate of mine, the other side of town, made exactly the same mistake you're making. You have to have the money make money for your living. This mate, he made a great mistake – lived off his capital . . .'

'Thank you Mr Bird I'm in a hurry today,' Hester threw the remaining grain and the basin hard in the direction of an elderly rooster. 'I am sure,' she said, 'that what happened to your mate is incredibly interesting gripping and horrifying but I really haven't time now. Katherine and I are going – '

'Miss Katherine all right, is she, after last night? Is she?' Mr Bird did not give up. 'After all that dancing?'

'Katherine is very fit and well thank you. She's cleaning the car.' Hester tried hard not to let the impatience, which she knew sprang from fear, show.

'I'll have a word with her then while you pop the kettle on. There's a thirst in all that dust and I wouldn't say no to a bit of coaxing to a scone if there's one going begging.' He had one leg over the fence. At the sight of the wires being pushed down even more Hester flinched. She was surprised to welcome the feeling of anger over something like a fence. 'No,' her voice rose, 'you can't see her just now, she's not dressed and we're in a hurry, we're going to town, we've appointments to keep and –' She tried to push Mr Bird back with her abrupt explanations.

'Anything I can do then? Can I give a hand?' he paused, one leg on either side of the wires. 'I'm not afraid of petticoats,' he added, 'you know that!'

'Nothing thank you. And there's no petticoat as you call it.' Hester tried a grim laugh.

'Ha! in the nuddy eh?' It was Mr Bird's turn, in the ritual of conversation, to laugh, 'Aw!' he said, 'you've very secluded here. Nice little neck o' the woods. You can do as you please here. Er,' he paused again his face close, opposite Hester's lips which were stretched across her teeth. 'Er,' he said again, 'no harm meant, Miss Hester. You know me. Just my little joke about the petticoats. You know me. All I want is to see you settled and comfortable.'

'Thank you, Mr Bird, now if you'll excuse me – ' Hester did not say more as, coming across the paddock was another dust cloud which rejuvenated Mr Bird's.

'More company.' Mr Bird, following Hester's gaze, turned to look. 'Just take a look at that dust,' he shook his head. 'The weather's over-due, for sure. Need the rain – that last little drop!' he dismissed it with a slight toss of his head.

'Isn't that your dust not settled,' Hester tried not to sound either impatient or hopeful. Another visitor now would be far from welcome.

'It's Borden,' Mr Bird said. 'I'm just come from there. P'raps I left summat.' He patted all his pockets as if making sure, Hester thought, that he had all his boring bits of paper. 'P'raps he's changed his mind,' Mr Bird was muttering to himself, 'or else I've left summat behind.'

'Good morning, Mr Borden,' Hester challenged as the young man drew up alongside. 'The gate's farther up. There's no way through here.'

'That's all right, Miss Harper,' Mr Borden called, 'I'm not stopping. I'm after someone. Any strangers about? Have you seen anyone? Had a man come yesterday. Said he wanted a place to work and I took him on, said he could have the end house, you know the one I mean and he said he'd be back when he'd fetched his wife and baby. Seemed all right, but to cut things short, he's nicked off with Rosalie's stuff. Diamonds, rings, the lot and a few other bits, worth quite a bit, all small stuff . . .'

'No, Mr Borden,' Hester's clear voice rang out. 'No one's been here. No one at all. But I'll keep a look out. I hope you find him,' she added. 'We can see a long way from here. I'll let you know if anyone comes.'

Mr Borden's thanks were lost in the roar of his departure.

'Well, if that don't bear out what I've been telling you, Miss Hester,' Mr Bird's pale eyes were watery with reproach. 'Borden doesn't keep cash in the house,' he said, 'if he did, it would all have gone too.'

'I really must go and get ready,' Hester said.

'Anything you'd like me to do before I go?' Mr Bird roused himself from inner reflections. Hester felt sure he could see the terrible theft from her own kitchen. He seemed disinclined to give up. 'What about that teapot?' he said. 'Why don't I see to the kettle while you just finish up on your clothes. A drop of tea, set us all right for the day.' He accompanied Hester towards the house. 'Place is looking very nice,' he said as if Hester was inviting him indoors. He seemed to be unaware of her lack of enthusiasm towards his visit. 'Oh! Ho!' he said, 'I see the old well cover's shifted. Wait on, I'll shove it back. Wind must a been strong in the night, especially here, I'll bet!' He leaned down and tried to pull the heavy framework across the hole. Hester, watching, saw his neck flush red and then darken to a deep purple as he tried, with all his strength to move it.

'Please Mr Bird,' she said, 'don't bother. We don't mind it being like that. It's always been like that,' she spoke quickly. Mr Bird, having failed, stood upright. Anyone but Hester would have felt sorry for him.

'Not as young as I was,' he mumbled, panting and wiping perspiration from his forehead. He needed to wipe his eyes too Hester noticed. She turned away. 'Mr Bird,' she said, 'I do have to go to town straight away, if you don't mind.' She paused.

'If you're sure, then, there's nothing I can do for you?' he put away his handkerchief.

'Quite sure,' Hester replied, 'absolutely nothing.'

'Orright. Good day to you Miss Hester, Gooday.' Mr Bird, as if ashamed now of his physical weakness, made his way back across to the fence.

Hester hurried to the house. It made her feel sick to think that someone, a thief, had been in the kitchen. As she opened the door she thought that she could smell the intruder. Perhaps every room and corner of the house was tainted. These thoughts and the knowledge of what lay at the bottom of the well took away any wish for the tea which was brewing in the patient teapot. She supposed this was what fear was.

Speeding along the long road to the town Hester thought of Katherine nervously sweeping the rooms and then, with thin tremulous fingers, moving and dusting the ornaments. She would do this and afterwards prepare the vegetables for the evening meal because she had been told to. 'Wash the spinach,' Hester had said. 'Be sure to get the sand out of it,' as she had often said. 'We'll have Eggs Florentine.' Katherine would, from habit, be very careful with the water and she would be sure to wash the fresh green leaves with a thoroughness equal to Hester's. Afterwards she would lie down on her bed because, as she left, Hester had said to her to lie down and have a nice sleep. The day, she said, was just an ordinary day.

As she increased the speed Hester tried to think of Katherine serene at home busy with simple household work. She tried to think of Katherine singing and dancing from one part of the small house to another. And she tried to picture her curled up asleep, possibly for comfort, in the middle of the larger bed which was Hester's.

Instead she knew the house was full of little sounds, footsteps and rustlings; someone breathing heavily; Katherine lying stiff with fear trying to hide flat under the tartan rug . . .

Hester felt hot. It was an unbearable heat. It was as if thinking gave her a pain. Her face flushed, burning hot. She rolled down the window swerving from one side of the road to the other. She felt a chill spread down her back. She knew that Katherine at home would be lying on her bed listening to the silence in the house. She would, very quietly, lean down reaching for her shoes and, with stealth, slip her feet into them and very slowly she would walk outside knowing that the house was empty because she has been through it with her little dustpan and brush and her cleaning rags. She has never before minded being left alone. Mostly she accompanies Miss Harper everywhere. Once when she was unwell . . . Hester smiled at the memory. Once when Katherine was unwell and had to stay in bed, Miss Harper, going off alone, had come back with the most darling duchess set. The dainty brush and comb and hand-mirror – Katherine still had them – were small and backed with hand-beaten silver.

'Oh Miss Harper, dear, wherever did you get them? They're so cute!'

'I found them,' Hester explained then, 'in that funny old shop, you know, near Mr Bird's place. The antique-furniture shop – the other end of town.'

'Oh Miss Harper, dear, they must have been terribly expensive!'

'Yes, but pretty Kathy, and I like you to have pretty things, especially if they are of good quality.' Hester smiled again. During the years they often tried to imagine the previous owner of the set.

'She must have been a princess, Miss Harper, dear, or a famous movie star.'

'Yes a princess or a film star. We do have them here in the wheat.'

Hester, still smiling, looked with approval at the familiar countryside. It appeared to be quite unchanged. How could paddocks, she thought, know when land changed hands. It was a fine day. If she stopped the car and walked perhaps she would feel safe and comforted. She always felt no harm, could come to her once she was on her own property. Now the property was reduced but the feeling of safety could persist, she felt, if she walked low down, small, on the gravel edge of the road with only the immense sky above her. But there was no time to walk. She increased her speed. The man on the track could mean that there was another. The other might be looking for the one . . . She tried to look with the interest of the landowner at the paddocks. It was not the same now. Perhaps, she thought, Katherine is out of doors, pleasantly warm in the yard watching the tiny clouds coming up from the west knowing that Miss Harper, who loves clouds, can see them too.

Without meaning to Katherine might go to the well, she might put her hand on the coping, from habit, to see if it is pleasantly warm to sit on . . .

No. No. No! Not the well! Hester's own voice in the car frightened her. No – Katherine! she croaked, come away from the well. Powerless and tormented with vivid pictures of Katherine standing beside the well, she thought of her alone and frightened; frightened at what they had done; Katherine alone hearing a sound from the well. Often there are sounds, soft soft noises, a rushing of wind and the drip drop of water when there is no water. Often they think they have heard water. They think they do hear water somewhere far down, drip drop, the soft sound of water, cool sweet water under the earth when they know there is no water. The well is dry. Katherine could be afraid that someone, a stranger is behind her; she might be afraid to look and, having to look, might glance round uneasily, peering squinting all round the yard.

Hester groaned aloud. She knew how unconcerned the poultry, busily scratching in the earth, would be. The geese, with nothing disturbing them, are quiet. They usually stand in little groups eyeing each other; lifting and stretching first one leg and then the other. They twist their strong sinewy necks and push their heads against their folded wings to smooth them. With efficient beaks they preen their feathers.

Hester, thinking of the geese, approved of them. It was a sign that they were healthy if they looked after themselves well. Katherine knows this; she reassured herself. All this wisdom and knowledge had been passed on to Katherine, she told herself. Katherine knew too that if a stranger came, an intruder, the geese would make a noise.

Hester bit her lower lip. She could not know whether the

geese were silent or not. 'I will try,' she said aloud, 'to count my blessings. I must discipline my thoughts. One blessing is that the truck is not damaged. He could have come up and through the windscreen but he didn't. We might all have been cut and bleeding.' There was no blood. It was a miracle, she thought and wished for a greater one. If only the whole thing had never happened. But it had. If only the whole thing could be done with. Finished. The man, whoever he was, Hester did not care, must have been caught on the edge of the bar. The better thing would have been if he had not been there at all.

Hester bared her teeth in a bitter smile remembering the flourish with which she had driven earlier from the yard sounding her horn and raising a cloud of dust in the track as if to obliterate for ever, for Katherine, every memory of the night before. She thought of Katherine alone standing by the well listening as if there was a singing and a moaning sounding from the depths. It would be easy to imagine a long drawn-out far-away sighing as if the wind stirred deep down in the earth and the sigh would be echoing a low voice from the well.

Hester gripped the steering wheel till her knuckles whitened. She clenched her teeth and tried to notice unmistakeable signs and details of other people's failure on their land. Anything out of order which she could pounce on to take her mind off what remained uppermost in it. Oh God! Katherine! She moaned aloud sure that Katherine would be too frightened to move away from the well. She tried by the force of her thought to make Katherine turn away from the well and to walk through the woolshed where the bagged poultry feed was neatly stacked next to the cheerful little stock of sweet-smelling hay. Katherine would walk on through the shed and out on to the track.

'Go back home, Katherine,' Hester said in the car, her face yellow in the rear mirror. 'There may be someone hiding in the saltbush.'

She must have been mad, she told herself, to leave Katherine by herself especially since they had no idea if the man had been alone. She wondered whether to turn back at once. She was more than half way to town. She thought of the rope. The rope and the money. The money. She must have the rope. Once they had the rope and the money the whole thing could be put out of their minds. It was only a question of not thinking, not remembering. She did not turn back. She studied the sky ahead. She tried to be pleased that there were clouds, even if they were thin, they were clouds and clouds were clouds even without the immediate promise of rain. 'Go home,' she wanted to shout across the paddocks to Katherine. 'Go in the house and close the door Katherine.' She knew it was not possible to walk far along the track. The saltbush pressing in on both sides would make Katherine feel she could not breathe and irresistibly she would be drawn to the open space of the yard and she would retrace her steps to the well.

Hester looked at her watch. It was only eleven. Katherine, if she did take a walk, would stay out only for a few minutes. Ten minutes would pass and it would be ten past eleven. The day stretched endlessly ahead.

It would have been better, Hester thought, to have taken the shorter way across her property. No, that was not right. Across Borden's land. She shook her head. That way she would have overtaken Mr Bird. She wanted to avoid him. It was not possible, she reflected, to avoid people in the country. Even where there were no people, people were about. The Bordens and Borden's men, they were bound to be somewhere between the dog-leg and the town. It was better to be on the road even if the journey took twice as long.

She tried to think of the dancing. She held somewhere in her head the exact music and the rhythm of the beat. She knew if she tried to sing she would only make a vague croaking sound lacking everything she wished for. She remembered Katherine's animated movements and the ripple of the light-yellow dress. She groaned. The dance was for her the only physical manifestation of physical love. Hester did not feel guilty about the feeling. It was private.

She pulled off onto the gravel for a few precious minutes alone on the edge of the great emptiness.

Afterwards, in her weakness, she cried a little and remembered again, all too quickly, the crazy ride, the dreadful thud, the man's body lifeless and Katherine's pitiable weeping. She wondered if there were marks in the yard which would give everything away. She should have told Katherine to sweep the gravel with the stiff broom. The body, though, had not touched the ground so there would not be drag marks.

The only marks would be those of the tyres unusually close to the coping of the well. 'I should have told you to sweep the yard Katherine.' Hester, again in her mind, saw Katherine loitering near the well as if drawn there by the sighing and moaning which they usually laughed about when they sat there together. If there was no sound from the well Hester knew, because they often did it, that Katherine would lean over the opening, which was larger now and more hideously ragged, and she would listen and, leaning still more, would strain to listen.

'Oh Katherine! Come away from the well,' Hester cried out as the truck rattled onto the road bridge. The river, far below, was undisturbed. The brown water had no ripples; it was low below the banks and stagnant. She drove straight to Grossmans. She would be as quick as possible.

Hester toying with the idea of a chain, never mind the expense, was told that it would have to be ordered and might take up to a week or ten days. She settled for a rope which had been her idea in the first place, the chain having only suggested itself as she drove down the High Street. A rope, she said to herself. There must be no delay.

'Ours not to reason why,' Mrs Grossman said to Mr Grossman in the back shed when she went out to ask him for a double length of rope, 'spliced extra strong', and to tell him that Miss Harper would wait for it.

Hester, weary on a little bentwood chair in the Grossman's store, listened to the latest news embellished with more details with every retelling, about the robbery at Borden's Place. So it is Borden's Place, she had to tell herself. She seemed to have floating black spots in front of her eyes. Her hands almost strangled her emaciated purse.

Without immediate money she was obliged to go to Grossmans where she had an account. In any case she did not want to drive further. Her main concern was to get what she needed and then to set off for home as quickly as possible. In her reserved way she did not explain what the rope was for though she was afraid Grossman would send down from the shed to ask so that he would know exactly how much she required.

On arrival, seeing some fencing wire in the side yard of the store, it occurred to her that it would be less questionable to order a roll of that. Wire, she knew, would be difficult to use. It would be better to ask for rope. If Mrs Grossman should ask her chattily what the rope was for she would say that she was thinking of hanging herself knowing that the people in the shop would laugh at Miss Harper's wit, accustomed as they were to her sharpness which often bordered on the severe.

Snippets of conversation sprinkled with *my dears* and *nevers* (the town was attracting artists and writers) reached her inhospitable ears – 'of course I told him that he absolutely *needed* the proscenium arch,' and 'I've got to prepare them for years of geriatrics – you see people all live so much longer now, these gels, d'you see, they come into their training with ideas about nursing handsome hernias and late circumcisions . . . '

Hester half listened. She would have given a greeting of sorts to a small bald man, a reverend doctor, if he had looked up from the revolving biscuit stand. He was picking up packets and studying them, one after another, as though some deep wisdom lurked in the lists of ingredients. She shrugged knowing that the finely printed promises were meaningless.

'They're getting some square plastic bowls in,' said a woman perched on the spare chair next to Hester's. 'An essential for the feet don't you think, but I see they haven't come in yet. Such a nuisance!' She stood up again displaying a restlessness not usual in a country store. 'I'll have to come back later,' she muttered to Hester. 'I'm writing a savage love poem and I've just got a line in my head. Frightened,' she said, 'I'm frightened I'll forget it. Cheerio!'

It was enviable this concentration on biscuit packets and this rushing home, needing to be back quickly, simply to complete a poem.

A silence fell on the shop as Mrs Grossman resumed her bulletin apparently interrupted by Hester and her request. The robber, it seemed, had actually been in her shop.

'Ever so pleasant spoken 'ee was,' she said. He had asked for a sandwich, she told them, 'his car was broke down just outside the town.' He was lucky, he told Mrs Grossman, to have got this far. He was going to have to go back to the city by train to fetch his wife and baby. 'Ever such nice people they are,' Mrs Grossman claimed more knowledge of the unknown. 'Ever such nice people.' The customers in the shop paused in the selecting of newspapers and magazines, their hands hovering uncertainly over cartons of milk and loaves of sliced, wrapped bread. 'He'd not got a cent on him,' Mrs Grossman's announcement accompanied the long-practised deft folding of pink ham in greaseproof paper, 'left his wallet, he told me, in the car.' She looked at her audience. ' "That was very foolish", I told him. I said, "Someone, not of this town, mind, but someone on the road'll be bound to stop by and help theirselves and take it. Not of this town," I told him,' she set her lips in a reproving line, 'but someone on the road travelling, passing through, as you might say. Ever so nice looking and got an education too, very nice speaking ways he had. Handsome. Well of course I said to him, "enjoy a bit of our country hospitality", I said. He had an appetite on him, I can tell you. See this ham? Well there's very little of it left and he must 'ave ett a whole loaf. And to think he must have gone through Bordens helping himself when Mr Borden's been that good to him, offered him a house and rail fares for him and his wife. I had it from Mrs Borden when she come in this mawnin' for her groceries. Mr Borden gave him the job and all found and then . . . '

Hester bored and afraid, struggled to her feet, scraping the small chair on the floor slabs. She was impatient for the rope. She wanted the rope as soon as possible please. She had a long drive as Mrs Grossman knew. Would Mrs Grossman kindly ask Mr Grossman if the rope was ready.

'Mr Grossman,' Mrs Grossman said, 'will splice all in his own good time. He's putting up some stuff for Bordens. Mrs Borden is calling back in a little whiles but Mr Grossman will do yours the very next.' She turned to her little audience. 'There I was,' she said, 'with a thief right here, just about where you're standing Mrs Harriot, I'd say just there between you and Mrs Skeine.' She bestowed the honour of the position on two customers who, clutching their sliced loaves to their breasts, exchanged the happy smiles and glances of the chosen. 'I could 'ave been murdered in my bed!' That Mrs Grossman's bed was in some more mysterious place above or behind the shop did not seem to worry either her or the audience. 'Yous'll all have to lock up,' she said, 'he's not been sighted. He's somewhere, you mark my words, nice spoken like that he'll be clever. Sharp as they come. I'll be bound!'

Hester, in her impatience, was hungry. Without shame she helped herself to a lamington roll and ate it whole. She was just finishing it and screwing up the wrapping when Mrs Borden came in. Mrs Grossman put her head through a convenient slot in the back door of the shop, 'Borden's order! Willy!' she bawled. 'Mr Grossman will be with you directly.' She came round the counter, on bent legs, anxious to enjoy once again Mrs Borden's loss of valuables. 'Was it your tiara, dear, that went?' she asked, her red hands holding her own flesh beneath which it was supposed her heart kept up its faithful beating.

Mrs Borden said yes it was her tiara and her solid gold rings and her brooches in marcasite and her emeralds and her pearls and then, seeing Hester, she said, 'Miss Harper, the very person I wanted to see, though I never expected you'd be in town today straight after our late late night! I'll come straight to the point.' Her clear loud voice filled the shop. Mrs Grossman forgot the contemplation of vanished jewels, perhaps at this very moment being valued, held, in the scrutiny of narrowed eyes, between the grimy thumb and forefinger which, despite their clumsiness, were capable of delicate restrained movement. She turned her attention to why Mrs Borden should want to see Miss Harper. Perhaps something dirty, private even, left behind and now discovered in the big house, her ears stretched in their eagerness.

'Mr Borden and I,' Mrs Borden said, 'are going to a wedding and I wondered if we could borrow Katherine for a couple of days, a week really? Do you think? I'd feel so much easier if she could stay in with the children. She won't be on her own of course. We have the yard houses full, well, practically full with married hands and their children, it's just, it's just . . . ' she paused seeing Hester stiffen brushing bits of shredded coconut from her black lap. 'You would be welcome too,' Mrs Borden smiled. 'It might be quite a change for you to stay in the old homestead again. We've had quite a scare, you see, the children don't want us to go. I wouldn't go away just now but it's an old friend from my schooldays getting married, we never ever thought she would tie the knot, she's . . . '

Hester, not wanting to even consider Mrs Borden's idea, having far too much on her mind, was wishing that she could get away from the shop and be on the road at once, rattling over the bridge and on towards home. She did not hesitate. 'It's not the kind of thing Katherine does,' was her reply, and 'neither do I', she was going to add, but Mrs Borden was rushing on, 'I hope you don't mind my asking. After all it would be nice, wouldn't it, for Katherine to feel she was earning some pocket money. Because, of course, Mr

Borden would pay ... '

Hester stopped listening. She sat like a piece of wood waiting for her purchase; her thoughts on the strength and the qualities of rescue in the rope. Mrs Borden forced a little grimace of a smile. She caught the gaze of one or two people in the shop and shrugged her shoulders. Mrs Grossman, opening the back door to give another shout in the direction of the shed, nearly deafened Mr Grossman for life as he was, with a load of bottles and tins, about to come through the door.

The relief of getting away from Mrs Grossman's endless talk and the added insult of being asked to pay for the lamington and the rope was short lived. With the road bridge and her own curt words of refusal (Mrs Borden) and a reminder (Mrs Grossman) that she had an account nicely behind her Hester was all at once filled with foreboding and dread. The quiet paddocks on either side of her did not provide the usual comfort.

Mr Grossman, muttering, had brought the rope from an obscure corner of his shed. It was coiled now, heavy and neat, on the floor below the passenger seat. Suppose the rope was not long enough or suppose the splice was inadequate. She had no right really, she knew, to send Katherine down, to force her to go down the well. Even if she were not lame, she would not want to make this descent herself. She had not really worked out either how to employ the rope. It would have to be secured firmly, she knew, to something which could not possibly give way. Wildly, in her mind, she searched the remembered walls of the woolshed, a metal ring or a post there would be safe but she could not recollect any such thing. And then the rope, to reach the side of the woolshed, would need to be longer. There was the block and tackle jutting from the gable of the shed but the rail was rusty and Hester could not remember ever seeing it in use. She dismissed it simply as apparatus belonging to a bygone age.

She pulled into the road house, *El Bandito*, for petrol thinking it was too far now to go back to town to her usual place. It was an irritation and an inconvenience not to have enough money. She was unused to restriction. She wished for tea, even for tea in a paper cup to take with her to drink later on when she had a longer distance between herself and the town.

El Bandito, the place Kathy was looking forward to visiting every night with Joanna; both girls dressed in their gear. Kathy had described in detail the clothes Joanna wanted; there was a navy-blue velour hat trimmed with grosgrain, a cloche hat pulled well down and to one side, a long straight navy-blue coat; 'she would have dead-white face powder Miss Harper, dear, and a blue chiffon scarf and no stockings Miss Harper, dear, but blue shoes pointy toes and thin thin stiletto heels and her lips very very red Miss Harper, dear, a deep red cherry red. Oh mint!'

Hester waited for her tea. The wheat paddocks came right up to the yard and up to the windows of the café. There was no other meeting place, she thought, except in town, and what there was would be the same as this. She tried to understand what it was which made Katherine want to be in this dreary place.

'Take a look at them two chicks,' Joanna had written a remark overheard by herself and a friend. 'Jeez, take a look willya, great pair of tits, d'ya reckon?' She was apparently relating compliments. 'And this fella kept shouting, "Want to go for a burn round the block?" Honestly Katt we didn't know! Whistled us all the way down to the gig. Stupid bastard, but. Wow! Great!' Hester tried not to let the words from Joanna's letter keep sounding in her head. It was the roadside café *El Bandito* which made her recall the unforgettable strange language of the letter. *El Bandito*, perhaps he no longer existed. A disposed of bandit. She shuddered remembering the heavy warm body and the difficulty of keeping lifeless arms and legs in line with the necessary movement towards the hole in the well cover.

She tapped the counter with her coin and the girl, at

length, appeared with the beaker of tea. Hester waited with impatience while a lid was pressed on. The café was deserted except for a blowfly trapped in the mesh of the net curtains. The two table tops shone with the sticky wetness from repeated wipings with an idle sponge. Hester almost bought a book from the stand of paperback books. The titles, suggesting escape, did not invite. She paused beside the cassettes, she would be able to afford one to take back for Kathy.

In her letters to Joanna, Katherine described in detail the road house and the drive to town but Hester was unable to remember what she had written. Joanna's letters were the more penetrating; 'Check that arse on it willya, she's got fatter thighs than me. Yuk! Imagine! Excellent!'

Hester almost saying these alien words aloud settled herself to resume her journey. The tea was propped safely on the seat beside her. She had, at the last moment, squandered the last of her few coins on a cassette, 'Buttoned up Beats'. She studied a few of the titles; 'I can't let you go' and 'Never Never Say Goodbye to me' and 'Hold me Just a little longer.' She smiled, in a twisted way, one of her little smiles.

Often in the evenings they played a game of choosing as two little girls, sisters, might play. While they were sewing or embroidering they took it in turn, strictly in turn, to select a piece of music or a song to play. The rule, unspoken, in the game was to choose as if for oneself but in reality the choice was made for the pleasure of the other person. So Katherine would make her choice, 'I'll have, Miss Harper, dear, I'll have Mahler, er, um *Abschied!*'

'Ah! that's a lovely choice Kathy. I'm glad you like that.' After the song of farewell, Hester, fingering a cassette, would take up another and say, 'It's a long time since I heard Neil Diamond, I'd like 'I am, I said.'

Sometimes the choosing was extended. The wood stove in the kitchen, after wanting 'All Things Bright and Beautiful' and 'There's a Home For Little Children Above the Bright Blue Sky' surprised them with 'I rage I melt I burn,' Polyphemus' aria from *Acis and Galatea*. And once, the Troll in the well chose 'Fifteen men on A Dead Man's Chest', a curiously unfitting ending tacked on to a Mozart divertimento, Hester thought, by the record company wanting to make use of the space for extra grooves on the record.

There was too the pleasure of the discovery that often the other side of a record or a cassette bought for a specific song yielded unchosen music which turned out to be even better than the one they had chosen. A surprise, a sheer gift, Hester would exclaim forgetting that the price paid was for both sides. And they would, for a few evenings, play the discovery to death.

Hester looked forward to surprising Katherine with the new cassette. It was impossible to imagine playing the game of choosing in the presence of Joanna. As she dismissed the ridiculous idea deciding, with her usual practical commonsense, that the game would have to be, as it were, put away during Joanna's visit, another thought crept in. They would not be playing anything in the evening unless the activities with the rope could by an enormous stretch of the imagination, be called a game.

Hester could still hear their argument. Katherine screaming and crying, 'All you ever care about is money. That's all that matters to you!' Katherine refusing and refusing to carry out Hester's request. Hester's order.

'The only thing you understand is money, what a thing is worth in money, that's all you care about.' Katherine's thin screaming was high pitched so that her words were almost inaudible, her voice sounding like an insect trapped in an empty lemonade bottle. An insect protesting, trying to say something but able only to produce the fragile whining buzzing sound.

'Katherine,' said Hester in a cool voice while Katherine was forced to draw breath. 'Money has its uses and you have shown no wish not to understand these uses. I expect,' she added, noticing that Katherine, after her dreadful screaming, needed even more time in which to breathe, 'that the double negative is too much for you. What I am saying is that you understand money well enough and that you, like other people, need money. We can't live without money.'

'I'll die then! I'm not going down there. I'll die!'

It was only hysteria of course. Hester, from her upbringing, knew that in matters of life and death common sense prevailed, especially in the country. Often something had to die so that something else could live and flourish. Like rotten fruit discarded, the dead man at the bottom of the well was not her concern. All they had to get from him was the useful and valuable thing which he had down there with him. The money. For a moment Hester thought of Rosalie Borden's jewellery. A grim little smile sat on her lips. If they found the tiara and the other ornaments they would keep them. That was too dangerous, she reprimanded herself, everything other than the money would be left. 'For the Troll, for you Troll,' she croaked. What they were about to do was all part of farm management. It was like getting a thoroughbred and possible prize-winning bull calf free from an injured or dying mother.

Hester frowned and swerved. She had the road to herself. She was content with the familiar dome of the sky. The uneasiness she felt in the road house was part of a general uneasiness whenever she had to leave her own landscape. When thinking of travelling with Katherine she knew she would have to make an effort to become acquainted with streets and shops which were not known. The idea of having a meal in a restaurant frightened her. It was something not in her usual routine.

For a time while she drove she amused herself, as she gazed from the stretches of empty road to the surrounding paddocks, with predicting failure for those city people lately drawn to 'getting back to the land' as they called this buying of hobby farms. These farmlets were selling fast.

Her comfortable contemplation of disaster for other

people soothed her and she began to think of the things she would do once her money was recovered.

Dismissing her uneasiness she thought how they would be able to continue with their plans and travel. One of the delightful things about travelling, Hester, dwelling in the past, reflected, was the food. Foreign places, foreign languages and foreign foods. There was a certain glamour attached to two soft-boiled eggs served, without their shells, in a glass delicately wrapped in a white linen napkin. This was how she had eaten her eggs with Fräulein Herzfeld all those years ago. She supposed customs like this did not change. After all, people with whom she had spent her life, had always eaten and still did eat eggs, two at once, fried on both sides and neatly perched on a juicy beef-steak.

In fresh surroundings Katherine would forget this whole horrible and squalid event. Hester smiled. The sturdy little Toyota was flying along, trustworthy and reliable, the distance covered without effort. Driving was a pleasure.

She thought of plays and concerts and the opera. With Hilde she had seen some romantic and beautiful performances. They, she remembered, in the ways of the Viennese had taken newspaper-wrapped parcels of salami and black bread to eat during *The Marriage of Figaro*. Hilde had been very fond of food. Still smiling Hester sustained herself with the thought of Katherine's excitement and pleasure as they were about to enter ancient and ornamental concert halls. She would enjoy too being one of the expensively and fashionably dressed people in the audience.

When Hester listened to music or when she read certain books she was able to forget that she was elderly and ugly and lame.

Sitting in the shop for such a long time had made her legs, especially the lame leg, ache. She had left the shop with her purchase unnoticed as Mrs Grossman was enlarging on her experience to fresh customers adding rape to the dangers she had escaped while in her strategically placed bed. The bald doctor was still in the same corner of the shop turning packets of biscuits over in his hands as if still trying to make comparisons and judgements; an intellectual exercise which Hester wished was hers. It would be easier to choose between biscuits, especially the savoury ones, than to go ahead with the macabre occupation she planned for the evening.

'I hope you don't mind my asking ... After all, it would be nice, wouldn't it, for Katherine to feel she was earning some pocket money.' It was not so much Mrs Borden's voice in Hester's mind now as the implication. What right had Mrs Borden to intrude in this way? Hester did not keep Katherine short, not at all. And then there was the earlier hint that Hester was preventing Katherine from growing up. The later words obliterated the earlier ones but Hester felt the pain of the accusation. She knew too, at this moment, that she did not want Katherine to go away. She loved her and wanted her near always as she was now. The thought of her belonging to someone else, 'tie the knot,' Mrs Borden said, was unbearable. People, Hester thought, who go to Church always want other people to go too. Vegetarians often tried to convert meat eaters. She supposed it was the same with marriage and childbirth. Women caught tried to ensure that others were similarly trapped.

Hester tried to dismiss Mrs Borden's vulgarity from the landscape. Realizing that she was driving too fast she slowed down and watched the crows flying low across the paddocks. She longed to get home. Part of the journey was this wish for arrival, for the serene peace of the yard and the quiet well-ordered kitchen. She found herself praying to a long-neglected God that Katherine would be reasonable and that tonight the whole horrible thing be dealt with, the money recovered and then put out of their minds.

In the distance she saw the line of trees which, her father always said, must thrive on an underground water supply, and which marked the farthest end of what used to be her property and where the dog-leg was. Seeing the trees even though they were a long way off reassured her. She would feel better once she was home. She needed tea, real tea not the stuff in the paper cup, and a meal badly. Katherine, after a rest and a sleep, would be baking a batch of scones. Her mouth watered. She wanted the sound of the kettle boiling and the warm safe smell of baking, cheese and bacon scones preferably, but mostly she looked forward to being with Katherine. The day had been unusually long. She never went anywhere without Katherine.

'Katherine!' Hester called on the threshold of the kitchen, 'A wet floor is not a clean floor. How many times have I told you that! A wet floor is not a clean floor!'

Wet patches amounting to small puddles trailing into one another decorated the usually spotless floor. There was no nicely spread table to welcome the exhausted traveller. Katherine gave no answering call and she did not appear. Hester searched the house calling and calling. This did not take long. She even looked in stupid places like the cupboard under the sink. Katherine was not to be found. Everything was tidy in the house except in the kitchen where it was clear that bread and meat had been cut up, in a hurry evidently, on the edge of the table. Bread crumbs and pieces of white fat, trimming from the meat, littered the floor.

Standing at the kitchen door she called Katherine again, her voice sounded weak and frightened. No answering call came from outside either. She could not remember ever before having felt so helpless, so frightened and so alone. She thought that Katherine, in desperation, afraid of what she had to do because she, Hester, was making her, had run away taking with her the weight of the dead man and the fear of the terrible thing she was being made to do. Where could she hope to run to. Hester regretted bitterly everything she had said.

The thick healthy rope lay in mocking ordered coils on the floor of the Toyota. Hester locked the doors, she had neglected to do this recently but felt strangely compelled now to take this precaution. She limped on her stick across to the woolshed. How stupid she had been! Katherine had gone in there and fallen asleep, tired out after the disturbed night, on the hay.

There was no sign of anyone in the woolshed. As she turned from the open end of the shed she saw Katherine.

Slowly Hester walked towards her. She was sitting, crouched on her heels, beside the coping of the well. She seemed to be huddled there, pressed against the stonework. She was perfectly still, her face turned away from Hester, as if she was listening. She did not appear to be hiding but Hester noticed at once that she seemed to squint sideways as she looked up, screwing up her eyes as a child does when he thinks that, if he closes his eyes, he cannot be seen.

'Katherine!' Hester moved forward as quickly as she could. 'There you are! Were you asleep in the sun?'

'Oh Miss Harper, dear, guess what! I'll give you three guesses. I've got a secret! Three guesses!' Hester, looking at Katherine, thought that she had never noticed before what a small pointed face she had. She was very pale, that was understandable after the events of the night. But this fragile bluish-white paleness was something out of the ordinary. It seemed to Hester that Katherine was illuminated from within in some way and that her paleness was like nakedness in the yard.

'Secrets?' Hester asked making another cautious movement forwards. She hoped Katherine was not going to be all nervy or go crazy or out of her mind over the whole unpleasant thing. 'Come into the house at once,' she said, her severe tones following naturally after the great depths of her fear. 'Come along. Into the house!' She knew it was imperative to be firm if confronted with hysteria. Like a mother who, having found her lost child, slaps him in the relief of being once more united, Hester was angry with Katherine.

'No kettle on,' she said, 'no baking done, the stove's black, no fire, nothing at all prepared for our meal. Where's the spinach I told you to wash, eh? What's happened to the cold mutton? What have you been doing Miss?' Hester only used the word 'Miss' when she was annoyed. 'Remember,' she said raising her voice from where she stood leaning on the door post, 'we have urgent work to get done this evening.'

Katherine drawn onwards into the kitchen stood facing Hester's anger; a small smile on her lips and her eyes bright as eyes with secrets are. 'I'm tired, I'll have you know,' Hester went on. 'I've not had a meal all day and just take a look at this kitchen. What have you been doing all day.' Because her own nerves were on edge she had to restrain herself from shaking Katherine. 'Where's the meat? And the eggs?' Katherine's reply shook Hester. Katherine said, 'I gave the meat to the man and I gave him the bread and . . .'

'What man!'

'The man down the well, Miss Harper, dear. He said he was hungry and anything would do. So hungry he said. So I put up meat and bread and apples in a plastic bag. He said to put it in plastic because of the water, in case he couldn't catch hold he said, in case the bread fell upon the water, he said, it's very damp . . . there's water down . . .'

'Katherine!' Hester's voice was deep with warning. But Katherine, smiling said, 'Oh, Miss Harper, dear, he isn't dead at all. I heard him. Soon after you'd gone I heard him. I heard him praying. He prayed 'Our Father' and he called on Jesus to get him out of the hole. Miss Harper, dear, I've been talking to him all day . . .'

Hester dragged a chair across from the side of the table. The noise stopped Katherine's speech for a moment. Hester sat down. She seemed unable to speak.

'He told me he was cold Miss Harper, dear,' Katherine said. 'He wanted blankets and a hot drink. I filled the thermos with tea. Real hot. He says there's water down there, Miss Harper, but trewly its got salts in it, bitter water, he says, a stream, he called it, trickling through the holes in the rocks. He says, Miss Harper, he's on a sort of rock and earth bank. He says you could call it a bank. And there's caves. He says it's very cold and he wants out as soon as ever you come back. Oh Miss Harper, dear, you do see don't you I didn't kill him after all!' Katherine danced across the kitchen. She filled the little kettle. 'I'll make us some soup,' she said. 'We could give him some too; I use the old rope in the shed to lower things down to him. I told him it wouldn't take his weight, that we couldn't risk another fall and that you were fetching a good rope from town. He said he would wait till you got back with the rope. I had a terrible time with him, Miss Harper, as he kept screaming, "Out. I want out", and I couldn't, for ages, make him hear about your trip to town. He's very bruised, he says, but not too serious he don't think. He might have broke his shoulder he says it's very painful. He can't understand how he got down there. "You're in our well," I told him. He can't remember where he was going or anything, he says he . . .'

'Katherine stop! Stop this. At once!' Fear. All the fear which Hester had often imagined could dissipate itself into the light gently moving air if she walked small and safe, low down close to the earth, along the road beneath the immense sky and between endless golden paddocks was in her voice when she spoke.

'Oh but Miss Harper, dear, it's trew,' Katherine's imitation American accent irritated Hester. 'Miss Harper, dear,' she insisted. 'Do come out and talk to him when you've had some tea, he'd love that. I've bin telling him all about yew.'

'Katherine! Stop all this nonsense.' Hester, though she had always encouraged the accent lovingly finding everything about Kathy charming and sweet, was almost screaming. 'Stop all this nonsense!' She raised her voice even more, against her will. She wanted to remain calm.

'It's not nonsense Miss Harper, dear, come outside and talk to him. I'll bring you tea out there. He wants to talk to you. He likes you heaps. He thinks you're great. The Greatest!'

Together they crouched, Hester as near to crouching as she could by the coping of the well. The familiar sound, a small rushing of air caught in the cylindrical shaft, came to them. They thought that faintly there was the drip dripping of a thin trickle of water somewhere far down. But, as before, this could have been imagination for it was, after all, a well. A place where the sound of water could be expected. They had often agreed about this.

Hester could feel the onset of a headache. There was a pounding in her left temple and a deep ache starting above and behind her left eye. The pain seemed accompanied by a feeling of nausea. When Katherine had made the tea and put a cup on a lace-edged tray cloth in front of her she had been unable to drink it. The tea, now cold, was on the low wall of the well.

They leaned over the ragged hole looking into the blackness but heard no singing or moaning or praying. The poultry were making their commotion before roosting. The noise, which Hester usually liked, annoyed her now. She sat up on the coping wall. 'Go and shut up the hens,' she said to Katherine. The well cover creaked and rattled and Hester struck at it with her stick realizing at once how ineffectual the ash plant was against the aged iron and timber. Katherine, shutting up the hens, disturbed the geese who were standing nearby with their heads folded back into the feathers of their wings; some with one with eye watchful.

They had to wait for silence before trying to listen again. It was already beginning to get dark.

'If you've been putting things down, where's the old rope then?' Hester demanded. She really wished to be kind and loving to the one person she loved but, whenever she spoke, her words came out in a sort of sharp bark. Her voice seeming not in her control. This in itself was alarming. She longed to take Katherine in her arms and comfort her. The girl was clearly deranged by the experience. Apart from being unaccustomed to taking people in her arms in order to comfort them Hester was not sure it was the right way to deal with derangement.

But Katherine was laughing. 'Why right here, Miss Harper, I have it all neat and ready. See? You can see it is all soft and frayed.' Sure enough in the shadow of the coping lay the old rope. Useless as she remembered it.

'That's not a very long rope,' she seemed to accuse.

'No,' Katherine said, 'and I didn't need all of it, not all the length there is. The well's not as deep as you thought Miss Harper, dear. He says that's the maddening part. He's not all that far down but to all intents and purposes, that's how he said it, isn't it just the sweetest way of speaking! He's got a beautiful voice, Miss Harper, he's had a very good education, he told me, to all intents and purposes, doesn't that sound grand, Miss Harper, he might as well be in the middle of the earth for all he can get out. He says a man can't even get up his own height if there's nothing to catch a hold of. He wanted to try this rope but I said it would surely give way and then what! I told him, all through the day, I told him you were buying a good rope. You have got it haven't you Miss Harper, dear, you have brought back the rope?' Katherine turned from the opening in the well cover to look at Hester and Hester saw in her eyes an expression she had never seen there before. 'I love him you see Miss Harper, dear, I love him and he says he loves me and he's glad I didn't kill him only knocked him out. When he's up from down there he's going to ask me to marry him and he says he'll ask you first, he'll ask your permission Miss Harper. Oh Miss Harper he's the sweetest sweetest person! When I threw him my blankets he said, you know what he said? Guess! Miss Harper, dear, guess!' She smiled, her teeth small and white in the dusk.

'I – I can't guess,' Hester almost choked.

'He said,' Katherine squirmed on the wall, 'he said he was cuddling my blanket, even though it had got a bit wet at one end, and kissing it because it had been near my body. Oh Miss Harper! No one has ever said anything like that to me before. It's, it's like being in a film and with me as the star.' She sighed and clasped her thin fingers. Hester noticed that she had revarnished her nails. She must have made time during the day for them.

Hester could see that she must be very careful, perhaps

even play along with the hallucinations. She checked an angry reprimand about throwing bedclothes down the well. She had, herself, thrown perfectly sound dishes down she admitted with honesty to herself. One, a valuable one, she remembered, had even been repaired years ago with narrow bands of silver and tiny jewelled clamps. For a moment she recalled the travelling tinker and his shifty eyes, eyes like Katherine's were just now, she thought. She wondered how Kathy could suddenly look dishonest. She had to realize that it was not sudden, that she had always dreaded a revelation of something not quite truthful. She remembered her grandmother thought the tinker looked sly and her father said that was not so, that the way he looked was the way in which he was being regarded. He said people often judged by what they feared or knew existed in themselves. He told Hester and her grandmother to watch the tinker when he was intent on his delicate work with the soldering iron . . .

Katherine was leaning over the coping calling in a soft voice which returned only the slightest reverberation. They, though straining to listen, heard no answering voice, no human murmur, no man's voice singing or moaning or praying. Simply the sounds of the hollow well came to them.

'I guess he's gone to sleep,' Katherine said at last. 'He said he ached dreadfully all over and his head hurt. I sent him down the brandy and the aspirin Miss Harper, dear, he asked for them and he said he would make himself comfy and wait till you came . . . .' She giggled, 'Oh Miss Harper,' she said, 'he said, know what he said? He said he liked the smell of my pillow. I threw that down too, he asked me, did I smell like that!'

Hester, who was astounded by the quality of Katherine's invention, said dryly with the hint of a smile, painful, because of her headache. 'Well firstly, he has no choice but to wait. As for liking your perfume that is perfectly natural isn't it, it is meant to be liked.'

'Oh Miss Harper, dear, then yew do believe me!' Katherine tried to hug Hester's awkward body. 'And I haven't to go down there after all because he can come up here.'

To Hester when she placed a hand on Katherine's brow it seemed hot. Katherine was decidedly feverish.

'There,' Hester said as soothingly as she could. 'There, there, Kathy. Come indoors to bed. We'll have to use the spare-bed blankets and pillow for you. Let's hurry! I have one of my heads coming on I'll have to get to bed and lie down before . . , ' she groaned and retched, 'before I'm sick.' She groaned again. It was degrading to be sick, especially out in the yard.

'Oh Miss Harper, dear, I am so sorry you're not well.' Katherine put an arm round Hester and walked carefully guiding the bent and limping figure across the yard to the open door of the kitchen.

In order to enforce some kind of order in Katherine's mind Hester, in spite of the malice of the threatened migraine, helped to clear the dishes from the supper she had been unable to eat. Katherine ate a great deal with unconcealed pleasure, Hester noticed, and afterwards seemed sleepy like a child. Hester felt that the discipline of sewing would help to settle them both. She wanted to do what was best for Kathy. Though almost blinded by the advancing head-ache she went with meticulous care though the steps of drafting a pattern and cutting out a tiny dress for a baby. Kathy had expressed a wish to make baby clothes so, Hester decided, that was what they would make for the fete even though, up to the present, Miss Harper's jam and pickle shed had not included them. It was true too that baby clothes always sold well. There was enough of the dainty yellow stuff left from Kathy's frock.

Hester, taking her hand from her throbbing head, guided the needle in Kathy's fingers to demonstrate the necessary regularity of the stitches for smocking.

'Just to get you started,' she said as kindly as she could thinking that tomorrow evening, without fail, Katherine must be made to go down the well to retrieve the money and, while she was about it, she could bring up the bed clothes and any of the dishes if they were not quite smashed to bits.

Yawning and stitching and admiring the effect of the quick embroidery Katherine laid it for a moment in her lap.

'Oh Miss Harper, dear, just think of it! I might be at this very moment making the first dress for my very own little baby.' Her blue eyes were very bright and Hester, thinking that her cheeks were flushed, said perhaps it was time to put away the sewing for the night. They were both very tired she said.

'Oh yes Miss Harper, dear,' Katherine's face disappeared into an enormous yawn, 'it's so cosy to sit here thinking about him. He must be asleep or he would have called up to us. I love sitting here having a rave about him. I shall so enjoy making my wedding dress, something simple with a square of heavy white lace over the bodice – and – d'you know what he said Miss Harper, dear? He said I must keep the old rope and have some of it looped round the hem of my dress. Isn't that cute?' She paused. 'And for you, Miss Harper, we could make something really splendid. Lilac! I know you prefer black but I couldn't have black at my wedding Miss Harper, dear, trewly lilac would be great. Do you think, Miss Harper, we could have the reception at the hotel like Mr Borden's party? We could have . . . '

'Katherine, Kathy' Hester's voice was abrupt. 'I'm going to bed. I have to lie down. Not well. Put out the lamp. Must go – bed –' the words jerked from her mouth as she clenched her teeth. 'Bed,' she managed one more word.

As the night wore on Hester, between bouts of dizziness and painful vomiting, was convinced that Mrs Borden had contrived to talk to Katherine during the party, putting frivolous and disgustingly flirtatious ideas into a head only too ready, being fed on romantic films and reading, for them. Mrs Borden probably suggested they come to town for the Bingo nights too. As if Hester had educated Katherine all these years for Bingo! And what if her clothes were a bit childish, they suited her and she liked wearing them. Hester wept in her pain and her trouble, silently. She faced the truth that she did not want to lose Kathy especially not into vulgarity and loss of innocence.

There was too the awful truth about a dead body pushed ruthlessly down the well. Something about this might emerge at any time. But even if it never did and she was, for the most part, able to keep it out of her mind, she knew it would return time and again. She would have it on her conscience for ever.

In addition there was the unthinkable prospect of Katherine and a wedding; not to be married to the dead man of course but to some oaf who was bound to come like a stupid and probably poverty-stricken prince (on social security, she almost snorted) into their lives. And who would, in spite of the great affection they – she and Kathy = had for each other, sweep her away, off her silly feet, to stock up his parent's miserable failing farm with children alongside the stocking up of his inferior cattle. All people, especially people like the Bordens, had only one idea in their heads and that was to make couples of people and to follow this coupling with reproducing.

The trouble with Kathy's prince would be that, now Hester had no land, a suitor would not come galloping from his father's rolling paddocks, only the unemployed son of a small farmer would come forward. Hester, almost moaning aloud, said over and over to herself she did not want a husband for Kathy. She was sure too when Kathy thought about it in her sensible way, she would not want to . . .

'Will Hilde, will Fräulein Hilde write to me? She will write won't she?' Hester asked her grandmother. The old lady dusted flour from her hands and began breaking eggs into a bowl. 'She will write? Say she will please.' Hester's fingers were white at the knuckles as she picked up the leather folder containing her writing things. She did not like her white bones showing through the skin, they were ugly, she would hide them in the pleats of her skirt.

'She might,' her grandmother pursed her lips, 'and she might not. Those sort of people don't write as a rule as there's nothing for them to say.' She searched along the dresser for the fork she used for beating eggs.

'Oh but there's so much for us to tell each other . . . ' Hester, seeing her grandmother frown, stopped speaking and tried to look pleased to see one of the dogs. Bending down, letting her case slide to the floor, she fondled the soft ears so that her grandmother should not see her tears.

When Hilde Herzfeld first came as governess to the little girl, Hester, she exclaimed at once that the child had the most beautiful eyes she had ever seen.

'Such large eyes, so deep, brown and thoughtful,' she said holding Hester's face between her rather plump hands. 'And the eye lashes, so long and the fine brow, very handsome!' Drawing attention to the eyes of her pupil took away any glances towards her ungainly movements. Hester's father had the same eyes though no one had noticed until Fräulein Herzfeld made the somewhat unexpected personal remark. He was very polite, perhaps shy, and always called Hilde Fräulein as she requested. Hester moved from his close companionship towards hers, and they were hardly ever separated until Hilde disappeared suddenly and the grandmother, without any real explanation except that Miss was ill and had to go home to her people, packed Hester off to a boarding school for girls of good families.

Hester, knowing what she knew then, or half knew, but clearly understood, did not persist with her questions. She learned early to avoid the unprofitable.

She realized quite soon that all the hours, after she, a little girl of twelve, thirteen, fourteen was in bed, belonged to Hilde and to someone else . . .

Hester, unable to sleep, turned over in bed. These memories, she thought, were squashed out of her life for ever. Whenever she told Kathy little anecdotes about her beloved Hilde Herzfeld they were happy little stories, the kind of thing Hilde herself would have related accompanying each little re-telling, as if bestowing charming little gifts, with nods and smiles and certain embellishments till there was an ever increasing merging of fact and desired fiction. This was not the case with this memory coming to the surface now with an inexplicable suddenness . . .

One night, Hester, hearing a noise, slipped from her little bed in the prettiest bedroom in the house and limped, without her special boot, along the passage, steadying herself along the wall, to the bathroom which she shared with Hilde. In the soft candlelight she saw Hilde crouched on the floor, her nightdress spread like a tent, red splashed, round about her. Hester had never seen her like this before and did not know that she had a nightdress patterned with red. They both had white nightgowns with ruffles of lace at the neck and the wrists. They made them together, Swiss cotton for summer and viyella for winter. Hilde, trying to be quiet, was crying. Hester saw that at once.

'Hilde! What is it?' The tall and angular Hester supported herself in the doorway; 'Fräulein Hilde, what is the matter?'

Long moans escaped from Hilde and a loud cry seemed to burst from her whole body. 'Ah! *Ach! Liebchen! Liebste* Hester. Go away from me *Liebchen*. Do not stay here. But . . .', she groaned again and seemed to fall forward to her knees under the nightdress. Hester, full of love and pity made an awkward movement as if to help her governess to her feet.

'*Ach nein! Bitte! Liebchen* – to go away. At once! I have to say your fazère. You tell him to come, perhaps, please. Tell him to come. I have to say your fazère.' Hilde's pain, it must be pain, her agony made her unable to keep to the perfection she was usually proud of maintaining when speaking English. *'Ach du meine Güte! Mein Gott!'* she cried out. 'Please dear Hester, go fetch your fazère. I must with him speak. At once! Go please! *Schnell! Ach,* what shall I do! My poor poor little Hester!'

Hester, staring at the blood-stained woman who was her dearest friend, knowing something of the scene already – never having been banned from the sheds and out-houses – began slowly to understand something dreadful. Without really telling herself that she could not reveal to her father what it would seem she knew about him privately, she limped back to her own room, instead of going to his room or her grandmother's. Climbing into bed she pulled the blankets up and round the top of her head. Towards morning she heard her father's car turning on the gravel outside her window. She did not leave her bed to peer out of the window but lay there listening to the car driving away until it was not possible to hear it any more.

Later when she sat at breakfast with her grandmother, the old woman did not offer explanations. She merely remarked that Miss Herzfeld had left sooner than was expected and that she would not be coming back. She added that arrangements were being made for Hester to go away to school, 'as girls did in books', the words began to pound like the pain of the first headache, the first sick headache, 'to go away to school, as girls did in books', her grandmother making it sound like a treat. She was already busy with the cakes and scones for the men and left Hester to console herself with the silky ears and the cold nose of one of the dogs.

'Fourteen,' her father said in the evening, 'might be a good age to go to boarding school', but she must remember that the other little girls will have been there for some time and already have made their friends. He was afraid, he said, that she might be lonely at first but he was sure she would manage.

Hester in her pain, remembering, felt now that Hilde, in the car, even though in desperate trouble, must have said something of this to her father. He would never have thought about it himself but Hilde, thinking as usual about Hester, gave him gentle words to pass on.

Girls of fourteen do have lifelong friends, Hester almost bit her pillow, and some do not, and those who have their friends do not want any intruders.

The tears Hester wept during the night did not relieve her headache. In her feeling of weakness she thought more and more of Hilde and how sweetly she was able to care and to cherish. How she sang *Stille Nacht, Heilige Nacht* without much tune but with unsurpassed tenderness over an earache . . .

Katherine came to Hester's bedside in the morning with a little tray of dry toast and tea. Hester, who had been dozing, had trouble waking up.

'Oh Miss Harper, dear,' Katherine's voice flowed like water, 'I've been out there since daybreak. He says even if he has to stay down in the well for seven years it will only seem like seven minutes if he can hear my voice. He . . .'

'Who? Who is here?' Hester raised herself slightly. She saw, when Katherine drew back the curtain, that it was bright daylight. 'Oh, close the curtains,' she moaned.

'Why the gentleman in the well Miss Harper, dear, he says he's sure I'm very pretty and he thinks you are too from the sound of your lovely voice. He says he heard us speaking last evening but was settled and did not want to get all roused up and, oh, Miss Harper, guess what! He says he thought I was only about sixteen and he's glad I'm over twenty-one for then we can be married without permission – people can marry at eighteen he says but he say's he's old fashioned and he's going to ask your permission even though he knows you're going to give it. That's the kind of nice person he is Miss Harper. I told him you would gladly give your permission for anything I wanted to do . . .'

'Katherine! Please! I am not well today. You know I am

not well.' Hester lay back on her pillow closing her eyes aware of the sourness of her migraine. 'I'll have to stay here,' she said. 'I can't get up.' She gave a little moan and, in a whisper asked Katherine to see to the fowls. Moving her head caused her great pain and the dizziness was frightening. 'I'll get up at lunch time, I'll . . .' she forced herself to speak.

'Oh of course Miss Harper, dear, I'll draw the curtains again. The light's too bright. I'll come back soon,' she promised as she tip-toed to the door. 'I must get him a lovely breakfast, he's saying he's dreadfully hungry.'

Hester alone in the dismay of her own illness realized that Katherine was really ill. Perhaps she would need to get a doctor, perhaps proper treatment of some sort would be needed to get her over the shock. Never, she said to herself. No doctor must come near. Katherine in that fake American accent would blurt out the whole thing. It was a pity that the accent had been encouraged, it had been a little joke between them, but now it played an alarming rôle in the representation of unreality. She would have, as they said in modern magazines, to see this thing through – by herself. She blamed the Borden's party but mostly she blamed herself. She hoped that Mr Bird would not come. It would be ludicrous as well as sinister if Mr Bird was to come round the side of the woolshed and find Katherine talking and laughing into the well. She would immediately pour the whole story out to him.

Hester tried to get up. She must get up. The terrible dizziness made her lie down again. She seemed to be turning over and over as the room itself was turning. She lay as still as possible and closed her eyes, trying not to notice the sickening effect of the affliction.

Katherine was at the bedside. 'Miss Harper, dear, how do you feel now? It's lunch time. Shall you want your lunch now?' The purring voice roused Hester. She tried to raise her head. 'I'll get up about four,' she said letting her head sink back.

'Miss Harper, dear, he wants out,' Katherine's hands

smoothed the sheet. 'He must come up, he says he can't stand it another minute. Can I let down the new rope, Miss Harper please? I tried the old rope Miss Harper but it broke, it's no good, it's rotten. I must have the new rope, you did get one didn't you Miss Harper. I must have it. Can I have the key Miss Harper to get the rope now?'

Hester was not expecting a direct demand. This was not the same as the day dreaming about being in love. The keys were on their chain. It reassured her to feel them next to her skin. 'Oh Kathy,' she said, 'not now.' I'm not fit for visitors. In a little while I'll be better. You know my silly headaches Kathy. When I'm better, Kathy not now.'

'We've had a long talk Miss Harper, dear. We have to talk; if we don't he says he'll be mad for ever.' Katherine kneeling by the bed smoothed the pillow. Hester closed her own hand over the little keys bunched on her flat breast beneath her nightgown. 'We had several long talks,' Katherine continued. 'He's very sorry Miss Harper, dear that you have a twisted back and that you have to wear a leg iron too, he wants to meet you real bad. I explained about the leg iron and everything so that he could know you real well. I do hope Miss Harper, you'll be better real quick. I'll tell him four o'clock then, four o'clock or as near as possible eh? Miss Harper?' The persistent little voice and the pattering of the hands on the sheet as if they were feeling for something was more than Hester could bear.

'I've looked everywhere for the rope Miss Harper, dear. Did you bring a rope Miss Harper? I must have it!'

'Let me rest a while longer,' Hester said. 'I'll get up at four o'clock. I promise.' She heard Katherine go from the room.

She had not finished going through in her mind her suffering over Hilde Herzfeld. Often she had tried to comfort herself by praying for Hilde.

She tried now. It was the only thing left to her knowing as she did know that she had slipped away, had avoided Hilde's terrible pain and loneliness. She had done something Hilde would never have done to her. Please God help

125 ☆

Hilde,

Our Father who art in Heaven
Hallowed by Thy Name
Thy Kingdom Come
Thy will be done on earth as it is in Heaven

This is the prayer Kathy said she heard from the well. Hester knew that she could not use this prayer for Hilde or for Kathy or for herself. She had been comforted at times during the years by thinking that her prayers could help Hilde in some way. But if the prayer came from the well . . .

She must have been dozing for Katherine was again beside the bed.

'Miss Harper, Miss Harper, dear, he says he's very sorry you're poorly and he says he's sorry he took your money. He wants out Miss Harper. I'm scared Miss Harper. He's going to kill us both. If we don't get him out he'll find a way out and then he'll get us both. Miss Harper are you feeling better? I've been all afternoon trying to calm him down. He says Miss Harper that he needs a better light than the torch and he wants better food. I don't know what to do Miss Harper, I wish you were well, I do really. He's had all the meat and the cheese and the fruit; he says he never touches eggs. Should I do a duck Miss Harper? Should I roast a duck? Would you feel like some roast duck? No? He says he must have oysters and a fresh salad as his gums are sore. I can't really do a duck Miss Harper because we don't have one dressed do we. And I can't get all that done and the cooking and stay by the well and talk and sing to him because that's what he wants, he says, to stop him going crazy. I can't get all that done before . . .'

'Katherine please. This must not go on!' Hester sat up and held her head in both hands. 'Katherine. Please. Stop this.'

'Oh but Miss Harper, dear.' Like an over-wound clock-work toy Katherine chattered on. 'You'll like him. Honestly! You will like him. It's only that he gets mad and angry and yells and shouts and uses language. It's then that I get scared, real scared. He's got a terrible shout, Miss Harper, and he know some words. Most of the time he's sweet. A sweety pie. I told him he was a sweety pie. I can't help loving him when he's being sweet. He's been singing for me this afternoon. He called and called while I was so busy in the kitchen. He said he'd sing for me.'

'Oh really Katherine, and what did he sing for you?' Hester asked, her weariness sounding like sarcasm.

'He sang,' Katherine said, 'something we know, something you taught me. He likes good music he says to tell you he knows a lot of classical tunes. He's been in lots of plays he says to tell you this too he's done practically everything there is to do in his life.'

'I'm sure he has!' Hester gave one of her little smiles which really only twisted one side of her face. Perhaps it was better to keep Katherine away from the well. She tried to think of ways of detaining her so that, so that, she stumbled in her thoughts, so that he might, if left unattended for long enough, die – again.

'This is what he sang,' Katherine said smoothing Hester's hair back from her sweating face, 'I'll sing it for you.'

Come away, come away death. Her piping voice was sweet and close to Hester.

And in sad cypress let me be laid
Fly away, fly away, breath;
I am slain by a fair cruel maid

'And then he cried Miss Harper and couldn't sing any more except for one line and it was this line: *My poor corpse, where my bones shall be thrown.*

'It's been a lovely afternoon Miss Harper, dear, I sat by the well with the sun on my back. If you could feel better Miss Harper, dear, you might like to walk in the air and come to the well too. Would you like that? You know, I'm thinking he's not such a young man either. He might prefer you to me. Imagine! I shall be jealous, but. Imagine! Jealous! If he does. Just a minute, I think I can hear him calling. I'll have to go Miss Harper. Will you be okay? I'll be right back.'

'Oh no Kathy don't go just yet.' Hester forced herself to prolong the conversation; anything to keep Kathy in the room, away from the well. 'Do you think he might actually prefer me?' she asked. Die! she said inside herself. Die now! she urged in her heart, knowing that one human being should not wish death on another. Die dead like you were in the night and stay dead. Oh God, she prayed wordlessly help me to help Kathy, Dear God if you exist help me. She did not move her lips but fixed her eyes on Kathy.

'Oh Miss Harper, dear,' Katherine laughed. 'I do believe you are getting keen on him!' She placed a little rosebud kiss on Hester's pale damp forehead. 'The only thing is, Miss Harper,' she teased, 'he wants children. Two boys and a girl. The boys first and the girl last. I said to him if he does go for you when he sees us both that you, being through your change of life, you wouldn't be able to oblige.' She giggled. 'But I did tell him you were good at adopting. And I told him at the Home there were lots of really little children.' She giggled again. 'Oh Miss Harper, would I be aunty to your adopted children? Or would I be a sort of cousin. I've always wanted cousins; Joanna has fifteen cousins. Imagine! Relations to go and visit! Would your adopted children, Miss Harper, be related to me? Would they?'

'I'm not sure Kathy,' Hester said as kindly as she could. It was one thing to read of these things in magazines and then, with common sense, discuss them with Kathy, say after dinner, when they were sitting with their sewing; to have such private matters discussed with a strange man was something very different. Hester was not sure what to say. 'Now,' she added a forced brightness to her kindness, 'if you'll help me, Kathy, perhaps I should try to get up. What a busy time you're having between the sick room and the . . .' Swallowing the last word she raised herself but had to flop back immediately as a feeling of nausea engulfed her.

Katherine disappeared as she poked under the bed for Hester's stout surgical boot and the caliper. Hester closed her eyes and gave herself up to the throbbing pain as it circled her head.

'He says,' Katherine emerged dusting the high rounded shiny toe of the boot with her hand, 'he says some women are in the change for years. His mother he told me was in her change for an age.' She giggled again.'Do you know Miss Harper, perhaps you'll be doing this too, his mother kept giving away her packets of you know what. That's how he said it, isn't he a sweety pie, he means pads. Anyway his mother kept giving these packets to his sisters, he had two sisters – they're both dead, so sad, anyway, when she'd given them away she'd have to ask for them back! Isn't he . . .'

'Be quiet! Katherine!' Hester said clenching her teeth, 'I'm going to have to lie flat for a bit longer. About an hour. I'll get up then. You'd better tidy the kitchen and see to the fowls.'

'Yes Miss Harper.' Katherine went with the quick little steps of the reprimanded to the door where she said in a quiet voice, 'Know this Miss Harper? I'm not going to give him up. Not for anyone!'

'Miss Harper! Miss Harper!' Katherine was pulling back the curtains.

'What is it now!' It seemed only five minutes since Katherine had left. Hester, opening her eyes, saw the change in the light. The afternoon was coming to an end.

'Miss Harper what shall I do about his food? There's hardly anything left at all. I haven't been able to get a thing done either with you ill in bed and him calling I mean hollering out all the time. I mean we could . . .'

'Calling is perfectly correct Katherine,' Hester interrupted in a cold voice. Perhaps that American accent could, with an effort, be corrected even now. Katherine was not beyond all teaching. 'Not hollering,' she said, 'that is not our English.'

'Oh yes Miss Harper, dear, I must say,' Katherine hardly paused for breath, 'he is trewly a kind man. I'm so glad I didn't kill him. I told him I'm glad I didn't kill him and he said he was glad too and that he couldn't wait to marry me. I told him we'd have a lovely wedding because you're so kind and generous Miss Harper, dear. We've been talking about our wedding. It takes his mind off being down there. I told him about our clothes. I described your dresses too,' she added.

'That was kind of you Kathy,' Hester said, unsmiling.

'Yes, Miss Harper I described all your dresses. I told him,' Katherine rushed on, 'I told him you had all those dresses in the wardrobe that you tried on sometimes but never wore. He says that makes him trewly sad and at our wedding you must wear at least two of them, you could change he says after the ceremony and then wear something else for the reception. Isn't that a cutey of an idea! He particularly wants you to wear the Princess Margaret tartan because of all the little pleats we made = it's a dashing dress Miss Harper, dear . . .'

'Oh Katherine = Katherine,' a moan escaped from Hester's tight lips. 'I've had enough of all this.' She wanted to wail aloud. Hilde! She felt the cry somewhere inside her but did not cry out. 'I know he's down there Katherine,' she said in the most sensible voice she could make from the suppressed cry, 'but it's a dead man we put down there and it is our money, you understand, our money that's down there with him and tonight you are,' she made her voice firm, 'you are going down there to get that money.'

Hester sat on the side of the bed and began to put on her boot and caliper. She felt ill and slow and clumsy. Katherine, kneeling, began to help her to dress. 'Miss Harper, dear,' she said, 'as I've said, there's no need for me to go down the well. If we put the rope down he can climb up to those metal rungs, you understand? Then he can climb out. It's so easy. Please when you're dressed let's go right out there and rescue him. Please. And tonight we can write to Joanna and tell her about the wedding and ask her to be my bridesmaid and tomorrow we can fix up a booking at the hotel and buy little invitation cards and . . .'

'That's enough Katherine,' Hester stood up and twitched her dress straight. 'Whoever it is down there is dead =

D.E.A.D. – dead,' she said, 'otherwise he would not be down there.'

'Oh no Miss Harper, dear.' Katherine's voice was soft like honey.'Oh no,' she said again, 'he sent this up just now for our shopping. He says he's sorry he took your money Miss Harper and he says to tell you here's a hundred dollars for you to go to town – he wants oysters. He doesn't mind tinned oysters seeing as it's the country.' She held out a crumpled note. Hester stared at it in disbelief.

'I tied the little flower basket to the old rope,' Katherine said, her voice seemed to falter when Hester did not take the money. 'Like I told you,' she said, 'it's only money Miss Harper, some of your own money.' She pushed the note into Hester's hand which hung as if without life at her side. 'I must fix us something to eat,' Katherine said and, with a nervous little laugh, she left the room.

Staring at the money Hester's first thought was that Katherine must be telling the truth after all. Here in her hand was some of the money. There had been a great many of these rolled up tight, secured by elastic bands, and tucked in the soft folds of the red knitted hat. She frowned and set her mouth in an even grimmer line. 'He'll stay down there,' she said to her dishevelled bed. 'If he wants oysters he shall have them.' Plans began to form in her mind. She would have to use Katherine to get the money from him. And when she had the money she would have to deal with him in the only way she knew.

Hester began to tidy her bed in a half-hearted way partly because she felt ill and weak and partly because her mind was busy elsewhere. She thought of the well and what it might be like down there on an underground bank of earth and crumbled rock. Dark and damp. Quite unimaginable and yet in her imagination she seemed to see the world of the well quite clearly. In ordinary circumstances there was a fairy-tale enchantment about the idea of secret streams and caves beneath the ordinary world of wheat paddocks, roads and towns. The streams would trickle through crevices in the rocks and flow more swiftly in channels and even through tunnels in some places. In the rocks themselves there would be faces of dwarfs and other fairyland creatures, there would be battlements and turrets of silent castles and little steps and slides leading from one cavern to another. Some caves might be lined with jewels. Her father had been right, as she herself had believed, about the underground water feeding the line of trees. If the water flowed down there finding ways through the earth and the rock then naturally there could be no water level in the well. He, the man in the well, had told Katherine there was water, he had said it was bitter. She suddenly stopped tidying her counterpane, irritatingly it was not on properly and, try as she would, she could not neaten it. She stood upright by the bed how could she even think about what he, the man in the well, was supposed to have said when he was not alive.

Another thought, an appalling one came into her mind. She remembered Mr Bird's warning. Perhaps he had been right after all. She could have laughed if she was not so bitterly hurt. Katherine must have the money. She had stolen it and now to make her believe that the man was alive had given a note back. Also Katherine liked food and knew that they would need to purchase their stocks of fresh food immediately (her trip to town had been solely for the rope), and so was prepared to give up some of the stolen money. She wondered what was the best way of behaving now. It was something that, because of the headache, was not easy to think about and do.

'Is your young man settled for the night?' she called in a cheerful voice aware, as she went down the passage, of the false tones. Katherine was bent over the sink.

'What, by the way, is your young man's name?' Hester settled herself on the edge of a kitchen chair? Her head throbbed but the ache was dull. She thought she was not going to have to endure a three-day migraine after all. Ordinarily this would have made her light hearted, full of laughter and on the point of doing something extravagant. Ordinarily too she would have been able to think with pleasure of a drive into town to replenish the pantry. It was stupid that on a day when she should have been fetching provisions she had spent the whole time in purchasing the rope. She thought now that she could fancy something to eat. It was clear that Katherine had not prepared anything tasty to attract the capricious appetite of an invalid.

'I asked,' she repeated, 'what is his name.'

'He says to call him Jacob,' Katherine said, half turning from the sink. 'He says, Miss Harper, to tell you to roll the stone from the well's mouth; he says you will know what he means.' Katherine dried her hands. 'Oh Miss Harper, dear, while you were fixing your bed he had a terrible fit, shouting and screaming. He says he can't stay down there another minute and he must be fetched up. He wants out, Miss Harper this very minute, at once. He keeps on like this and when he's up he's going to get us, kill us he means it he says. And then straight after he cried and begged my pardon and yours too of course and now he says he didn't mean a word of what he'd said. He says it's because he gets this terrible hopeless feeling down there Miss Harper.' Katherine was very white faced. Hester noticed too that she trembled. 'Miss Harper,' Katherine said, 'he's hit his head on a rock.' She paused. 'On purpose, Miss Harper, because he's losing faith, he says, in the milk of human kindness and he's scraped all the skin off his hands . . .'

'I asked you,' Hester interrupted, 'if you had settled your boyfriend for the night because, if you have, I think that I deserve a little attention after my headache.'

'Oh yes, of course Miss Harper, dear.' Katherine was concerned. 'What could you fancy Miss Harper, dear, I could . . .

'Do my hair first Kathy please,' Hester said in a complaining tone, 'and then I'll try some toast and perhaps an egg.'

Katherine brushed Hester's long hair. With gentle patience she began to untangle the knots. Because of feeling ill Hester had not put it in a net before going to bed. Katherine pressed the hairbrush in long slow sweeps downwards and then, dividing the hair, she began to plait it.

133 ☆

Hester, partly soothed, began to feel irritated as she felt the thin, nimble and, as she thought, thieving fingers moving over her scalp and in her hair.

'Come along, don't be all night!' she jerked her head. In reply it seemed that Katherine made an equally impatient movement with the brush tugging unnecessarily at a tangle. Hester felt at once that this answering impatience was an indication that Kathy had stolen the money and thoughts of possession gave her an upper hand. It was, she thought, the feeling of ownership, even if wrongly achieved. She, Hester, would soon show Katherine that the time of being in possession would be brief.

It was painful to know that Kathy could steal from her when, during the years, she had loved and cherished her possibly more than a mother or an aunt might. It had always been taken for granted that Katherine loved Miss Harper. This was what their lives together had been and it was shown in all sorts of little ways.

The dead man, the intruder, had distorted their relationship. He had brought disaster and a remedy must be found.

'Kathy you're plaiting too tight, much too tight, stop pulling do! It'll make my head worse. You know that!' Hester, disliking her own voice, put her hands up to hold her great lengths of hair. There was no point in a remedy when faith between them was lost. Money was the only answer.

'Kathy,' she said, still holding her hair against the pull of the plaiting, 'would you like some investments of your own?'

'Why yes Miss Harper, dear, if yew think that's best,' Katherine replied in a purring voice.

Not even a 'thank you', Hester thought. It must be because she felt secure enough with the stolen money or it might be that she did not fully appreciate that she was being offered a considerable amount of money to be her own for ever. Hester thought to carry the test even further.

'Tonight,' Hester said, 'you will go down the well on the rope I bought and when we have the money safely here in the house – tomorrow I shall take you to town and we'll invest that amount in your name. And then for our living expenses and for our holiday in Europe I can draw out . . .' She paused, waiting for Katherine to confess in the face of such generosity that there was no need to make the horrible descent – that the money was there already in the house. Hester was prepared for Katherine to be triumphant. They would celebrate together the presence of the neatly rolled-up notes.

Katherine did not reply at once, her mouth was full of hair clips. Hester, waiting and feeling the clips sliding on her scalp, allowed herself to wonder when Katherine could have taken the money. Any time, she supposed, possibly just before they left for the Borden's party. It might, it would surely be hidden quite near, somewhere in the house, perhaps even under an upturned jug or a basin on the dresser. Hester glanced quickly round the kitchen. She wanted to jump up and pounce on an inverted bowl and turn it up with a definite movement of discovery and reveal the hidden treasure. She had to restrain herself knowing that Kathy, accustomed to her own ways, would use hiding places which she herself would choose. The red hat, she noticed, lay inside out, empty on the shelf where it was always kept. The sight of it made Hester's heart pound with suppressed anger. She said nothing and waited for Katherine's reply.

'There's no need Miss Harper, dear,' Katherine said smoothly, 'for me to go down. I've already explained to you, if you'll let me have the key to the Toyota I'll get the rope – it is in the Toyota isn't it? – and we can let him climb up. He'll be a lot better than me at climbing on a rope! Miss Harper, dear.' Katherine's voice changed. 'He can't go on being down there. He'll go mad. He's told me he'll go mad and besides he's got some injuries. He's in pain and he wants a doctor and he's told me he must out tonight. I must get the rope off you; he's told me I must. He's afraid Miss Harper, dear, don't you understand it's awful down there and the torch batteries are low and I've had to tell him we haven't any more. They're our last I've had to tell him. He says I must get the key off you. I've told him you keep them on that chain around your neck he says I'm to get it off you . . .' There were tears not far away, Hester knew the sound.

'If we get him up, your young man,' she said in an easy bantering tone, 'he'll just as soon put us both down there. You can believe me, Katherine, anyone who comes back to life after being killed by a truck and thrown down a well isn't going to take things lightly. Understand this, Katherine, once and for all, you have to go down tonight and retrieve the money.'

'Miss Harper, dear,' Katherine seemed to croon, 'yew don't believe that he's really alive, do you. Well, I'm telling yew he is. I've been all day out there, he doesn't like being left alone. I should be there now only I can't be in two places. . .'

'If he is alive as you say he is,' Hester interrupted continuing in the light teasing way, 'just you make yourself nice and clean and pretty, put on your yellow dress and some of that exotic *Chloë* and go down to him. You know, offer yourself to him – since you love him so much it shouldn't be too difficult. Tell him you love him, that you want to bear his child and ask him for the money, tell him to trust you, promise him everything and so on and so on, you know the kind of thing. And you also know that lovers often break promises. So, what's the problem? Hm? But,' she added, 'it's much easier to get money from a dead man. Much quicker too, you'll be down and up and it will all be over and done with. Now,' she said, 'time to change the subject. I think I could eat an egg. What about you? You'll have an egg too? I'm going to have two, lightly boiled and scooped out into a glass and I'll have some thin slices of freshly buttered bread.'

'Miss Harper, dear,' Katherine said, making no move towards the preparation of the food. 'Do you remember,' she said in a quiet voice, 'do you remember he sent up a note, a hundred dollar bill?'

'Yes yes of course,' Hester said, 'one of mine I believe.'

She limped across to reach for the special little saucepan they used for eggs.

'Miss Harper, dear,' Katherine said, 'I couldn't have had that if he hadn't sent it up in the little basket. I never have any money so how could I have that note?'

'Katherine!' Hester barked, 'do not continue to lie to me. If you would like to have the money you have taken and invest it for yourself I am perfectly willing for you to have it. I'll discuss it with you later. Now we must see to our supper or whatever this meal is, if your gentleman friend has left us something in the larder.' She hummed a song tunelessly, a subdued braying resonant in her nose.

'Money is the only thing you know or care about.' Katherine's voice caused Hester to turn so quickly that she almost lost her balance.

'Money money money,' Katherine shouted.

'Yes Kathy, dear, money,' Hester said, 'I do know about it and I care about it and so do you obviously. Oh Kathy,' Hester said, her face changing, 'Kathy, what's the matter with us.' To her surprise and in spite of her intention, she began to plead. 'Kathy,' she said, 'Kathy listen to me, there's only one person I really care about and that's you and the one thing I care about is your future and your enjoyment in life. You know that. I've never been mean to you. I've always tried to please you and I've always trusted you completely. Doesn't all this mean anything to you at all. You must know that you are the only person I live for.'

At this Katherine burst into tears and cried aloud. 'Oh Miss Harper, dear, you are good to me. I know. I know but please don't let's leave him one more awful night down there. It's hell he says. I can't rest Miss Harper, dear I haven't slept and I'm so tired but I can't bear to be comfortable knowing that he's all alone in that dark wet hole. Miss Harper, I've spent every minute I could out there with him telling him over and over that you are a good kind person that you'd give me the key and I'd get help to get him out. I keep talking to him telling him everything'll be all right. Please Miss Harper, dear, just give me the key to the Toyota, please. You see if he can't climb up the rope himself we'll have to fetch help. I promised him we'd fetch Mr Borden and some others to help.'

'Stop that noise at once,' Hester said in fear. She held one hand to her flat breast and was partly reassured. She could feel the keys safely in their place. 'Stop all that rubbish!' she said determined to squash the outburst of hysteria. 'Get on and spread the bread and butter, nicely too. I don't want the bread all broken and the butter in lumps.'

'It isn't rubbish,' Katherine shouted, 'and I'll tell you this, Miss Harper, I didn't kill him. I did not kill him and it was you that put him down the well. It was your idea and you did it and if you keep him down there he'll die and you'll have been the one who killed him. You can't kill him! Give me the key!' she screamed. 'I've got to go and get help. I hate you!' Her scream rose higher. 'I hate you and I shall always hate you. I see now what you're really like. Don't forget I had all those years in the convent. We didn't just talk about nothing there. I do have something. I do know what's good and what's not good – I know a bad thing. Miss Harper I know when a person's bad.' She drew breath. 'I hate your music too. More than anything I hate that.' She sat down at the table and cried.

'Kathy,' Hester said, her hand outstretched as if she would stroke the fair head. 'You realize don't you that I put the body in the well to save you. You understand that surely. I got rid of the body, of the evidence. Have you thought of that. Now listen, why can't we calm down and just talk quietly . . .' She limped round the table.

'Oh rack off!' Katherine jerked herself away from Hester who was about to caress her shoulder. 'Piss off!'

The two women, as if unable to leave each other, sat in the kitchen, one each side of the table where the partly prepared meal remained. Neither of them attempted to eat anything, not even a piece of bread. Neither of them spoke. From time to time Hester rose awkwardly and, limping to the wood box, she put a piece of wood in the stove. Outside it had started to rain. Long overdue the rain was heavy and persistent. They heard it beating on the roof. Water ran in long rivulets down the outside of the uncurtained kitchen window. The fragrance of the rain on the dusty earth which normally pleased them both was not mentioned. It was as if they had not noticed it.

Katherine said once, 'Please Miss Harper, dear.' Hester, knowing the need not to give way to hysteria, did not reply for a time. 'Get ready for bed Katherine,' she said later.

Neither of them attempted to move away from the table. Hester sat upright on her chair, her usually busy hands were idle. No knitted garment was taking shape on her lap. Katherine stared at Hester until tears filled her eyes and she was obliged to wipe them away. Sometimes she rested her head on her arms on the table. Raising her head Katherine said again, 'Please, Miss Harper, dear, the key to the Toyota. Let's go out to him.'

'No it's raining too much,' Hester said, adding 'I told you to get ready for bed hours ago.'

Slowly Hester began to understand that Katherine would wait until, exhausted, she had to sleep. She often, after a bad headache, had a long and refreshing, almost childlike sleep. She understood that this was what Katherine was waiting for and then her light fingers would quickly unlatch the key from its accustomed place of safety. In the face of determination, Hester knew, nothing was safe. All the same she resolved not to sleep. Kathy had not slept and she, Hester almost smiled, because she was young was capable of hours of very deep sleep.

Sometimes Katherine cried softly to herself, her face hidden in her arms and, at other times, it seemed that she did sleep for short intervals. Hester, alerting herself, understood too that Katherine might pretend to be asleep so that Hester, feeling relaxed, might go and stretch out on her bed where she would the more easily sleep.

The rain continued. It had danced on the roof to start with, rushing with a musical sound along the gutters and into the dry downpipes. Then as the downfall increased there was no other sound except that of the rain which became a torrent thundering on the safe roof of the cottage. At times Hester gave herself up to the sound of the rain. She thought about the places on her father's land where water collected and flowed. It seemed, as she grew older, that like the many unblemished summer days remembered there were, in her childhood, very many wet winters. A great deal more rain.

'Come Hester!' Hilde Herzfeld said. 'Let us make a little rain walk.' They went out together in their rubber boots. Hester unable to wear wellingtons on both feet kept her special boot as dry as she could. That had been quite a game, something Hilde invented. She would go first to test the safe places on the soft wet tracks. 'Come Hester, here is an island!'

Strange water courses reopening altered the paddocks. The rain altered life too. Everything began to be active with the coming of the rain. People changed too. They rejoiced and they forgave old bitterness. And they did optimistic things like sowing more land and increasing their buying of machinery. Even her grandmother, who did not allow boots indoors, did not seem to mind mud on the kitchen floor when the men came in to devour the date and walnut cake and the scones freshly baked and piled with red jam and cream.

When she lay in bed long ago she heard the rain in the night, a steady drumming on the roof and a waterfall over the eaves when the pipes could not take the flood. All night long, behind the noise of the rain, chairs and tables talked and groaned and the floorboards, creaking, passed the sighs and the whispers from room to room and on up into the timbers of the roof. Sometimes something cried out. There was a pain and she called out. Her father came flickering across the ceiling in the light of the candle he carried on a saucer. It was the mysterious cramp in her lame leg or an earache. Later, during the nightmare, as her father and Fräulein Herzfeld hurried along the passage, the double light from two separately held saucers flooded Hester's ceiling and their two shadows, grotesque and tremulous, moving up and down and across the walls, colliding, became one. Her father, yawning, told her stories in a deep voice about the great red fox and brother wolf . . .

Sitting in the kitchen, jerking herself awake, Hester listened to the rain. She longed for the free pleasure of the rain. Everything would look different in the morning but the problem would be unchanged. On the other side of the table Katherine was perfectly still. Hester wondered if she would be better before Joanna came. The thought of the impending visit was unbearable. In a tired way Hester began, in her head, to compose a letter in which she suggested that the visit be put off 'for a time'. 'Katherine is not well . . .' Should she get some decorated note paper? . . . Joanna would be sure to want to know what was the matter, the two girls having grown up together seemed closer than some sisters Hester had known. What sort of thing could a young woman be suffering from so that an unwanted visitor could be discouraged. Something infectious – measles, mumps, chicken pox – but there were all the childish illnesses probably shared already by the two girls. Appendicitis, also belonging to childhood, and a hospital would be required and Joanna, like a great many people, would love hospital visiting. A nervous breakdown, a convenient phrase, but someone or something would have to be explored and explained and blamed . . .

One of the red fox stories her father told was about the fox who called out at intervals, *'Top Off, Half Gone'* and *'All Gone.'* There were times when Hester felt she was on the edge of a memory which was about to be revealed. And then suddenly there was no revelation, only a closing off of the memory. Why did the fox call out these strange names?

Somewhere in her mind Hester remembered the fox was a mid-wife but this only added to the mystery of his shoutings.

There were a number of things she liked when she was a child; especially there were words; *I challenge thee to mortal combat!* She said it to everyone. Fräulein Herzfeld blinked her slightly bulging eyes. 'Vot iss ziss?' she said, not understanding. *I challenge thee to mortal combat!* Hester, striking an attitude, waved her umbrella spear.

'Bott it iss not rainink Hester!' Hilde went on reading and Hester, as usual, thrust her spear into the sofa cushions . . .

The fire was almost out in the stove. Hester rose with stiff awkward movements and put in some small sticks. She hated a black hearth. The kitchen was cold. She had been, she supposed, thinking of Hilde Herzfeld. Together they had played surprisingly childish games. On going to the boarding school she had had to 'be her age' as Rosalie Borden would say. With Hilde, Hester felt safe and young and happy. Perhaps now she had been making an extension of this youthful happiness in her attempts to give Kathy a home and to educate her at an age when most people considered themselves, as Kathy and probably Joanna would say, 'through with school'.

It was still raining. Water levels would rise. Hester thought with satisfaction of the tanks and the dams and dismissed the thought at once since they were no longer hers. She thought of their own tank filling and wished that it was the only thing she needed, during this long night, to think about. Katherine still had not stirred from the dark side of the table. She must have been unable to keep her vigil. The keys were still on their chain. Hester stroked them with cold grateful fingers. She must have fallen asleep for a short time. Katherine, with that youthful ability to sleep anywhere, slept on, her head resting on her arms on the table.

Hester moved on her stick across the kitchen and fetched the tartan rug which she placed gently on Katherine's back and shoulders. Leaving the kitchen once more she felt along the shelf inside her bedroom door, in the dark, and selected a book. She knew without a light which book it was.

The smell of the book reminded her of her room in the old house. Her window there looked out across the pasture which came right up to the house on that side. The sheep were often there especially when there were lambs. Often she sat reading half hearing lambs bleating and the gargling choking replies from the ewes. Sometimes they were close beneath her window and seemed to be in the room with her . . .

She took the book back to the lamp light on her side of the table. She began to read.

. . . a sweet rural bower roofed overhead with an arch of living boughs . . .
and:
. . . when they had been gone a year, Telephassa threw away her crown because it chafed her forehead, 'It has given me many a headache,' said the Queen, 'and it cannot cure my heartache.'

The Queen and her sons, Hester remembered, were travelling endlessly and endlessly searching. She turned the pages with impatience to find the artist's audacious embellishment of the myth. Of course there were no pictures. In her mind she had made them from the words. She put aside the book and prowled once more alongside the dark shelf. She brought back to the table the shabby copies of *Silas Marner* and *Robinson Crusoe*. She must endure the night. And the day and the next night. Her head felt as if in a tight crown. It was the tight plaiting of her hair. 'Katherine, the plaits are too tight.' She said the words in a low voice. Her own hair was bringing back her headache.

Usually she felt better when it rained. She would be better in the morning. She wished for a miraculous recovery for Katherine.

Cherishing, safety, human efforts towards love and faith,

that was why she liked to read about the lonely old weaver, the miser, an old man caring with tenderness for the motherless child.

The stone hut was made a soft nest for her lined with downy patience . . .

She read for a time and then opened the other book. Once, when she was a child, she had killed a meat sandwich. She had then her own pallisade, built by herself of hay in the barn. And every day she went out from there to hunt. She took the hunted sandwich to bed in the pocket of her nightgown and wrote in her diary: *I went out into the island with my gun to see for some food . . . I killed a she goat . . .'*

She knew that fate left no margin for choice about islands and survival.

There was a high wind now. It seemed to howl round the cottage. She thought about the safety of her roof knowing that it was well made. The yard too was well fenced, she had insisted on that, and the old woolshed had weathered many gales. At times, behind the noise of the wind she heard the lift and fall of the well cover. As soon as this storm was over, she told herself, she would have that cover replaced and the well closed over properly. She blamed herself for Katherine's present hysteria = for that was what it was.

The fantasy created over the years contained in its invention all that was romantic and beautiful; the fairy-tale lovers and the safe dangers of cosily imagined evil lodged in some distant place. There was the idea of a world of caverns lined with jewels and perhaps the possibilities of magic practices which made wishes come true. There were the sounds too of the rushing wind, the dripping of precious water and the unintelligible murmurings of voices, which could be human, in the depths of the well.

One of the memories of the wind and rain years ago was that carried in the noise of the storm was the human voice. It seemed to cry from the top gables of the house or from some remote corner, a sheepfold long out of use, or from the banks of the creek which had, over the years, carved for itself a gully so deep that it was a ravine down which the black water, in flood, poured.

During a lull in the gale Hester was once more enveloped in her fear. She shivered with an intense cold and she had to clench her teeth against waves of nausea. She thought she heard a voice somewhere outside. She thought someone was calling and calling. She thought of her gun and wondered where it was. The wind rose raging once more and the voice was lost. When the wind dropped more rain fell and all sounds, real or imagined, were engulfed in the noise of the downfall. She sat tense on her chair. Her head throbbed with the remnant of the migraine. She touched her head with tentative fingers; her hair was drawn painfully from her forehead. When she looked at her hands the bones of her knuckles seemed to shine white under her skin.

She stared at the open book without reading. A piece of charred wood stirred in the stove. She jerked round as if to see who had entered the room not in an ordinary way but with stealth. Katherine still slept, her head resting on her arms on the table. When she looked at the clock Hester saw that it was not even midnight. So many hours to wait till morning. In an attempt to control her fear she tried to look forward to the morning, to the sun rising over the storm-washed land. The morning, she knew, would not solve. It could only complicate. She got up slowly to attend to the stove. There it was again, she was sure, the voice in the wind calling. She paused, leaning heavily on her stick, to listen. It could be an animal she told herself. All kinds of birds and animals made human noises, especially sheep when they coughed. There was no sound except the steady pouring of the rain. She finished making up the fire. In the morning, after the storm had blown itself out, everything would seem different. She would be able to smell the wet earth and feel the fresh air on her face. It would all be over, that trouble out there. Whatever was making that noise would no longer be making it. It would all be over, she told herself, knowing that it could not be.

She understood that Katherine, while brushing and plaiting her hair, had hoped to slip the keys from their safe mooring. Her plaits were too tight. She would have to undo them herself even though the exertion of raising her arms would bring back the migraine.

'Kathy,' she wanted to say, 'wake up, let's be friends. Undo my plaits please, they are too tight. Kathy please. Please let's forget all this trouble and go on the way we were, Kathy.' She found herself composing explanations; 'Kathy I thought I was protecting you by doing what I did = but I must tell you = people would have been sorry for you = but I didn't = I don't want people here, I don't want newspaper men and photographers or journalists and sightseers. I don't want other people coming here poking about in our lives. Kathy I want to tell you this so that we can go on the way we were.' How could she say these things to Katherine? 'Kathy if I hadn't done what I've done we would have the money now.' If she understood herself like this, Hester thought, perhaps she could make Katherine understand too. But there were other things . . . How could Kathy discuss with a strange man the private things of life, of her life, Hester's, as she had done? It was all right to read about these things in a magazine article which was accompanied by a photograph of a mature and neatly dressed nurse. Hester and Katherine with a wonderful unrestrained freedom discussed together all the problems they read about. Katherine knew a great deal more than Hester. Hester, supposing that the convent education was more comprehensive said so on one occasion. Katherine laughed. 'Oh Miss Harper, dear,' she said, 'at the Home they could only think about one thing. They were always looking and sniffing to find out if there was an unwanted baby on the way!'

Hester realized she must have been asleep. The lamp was out and the kitchen was dark except for a small glow from the stove. She could just make out that Katherine seemed to be no longer sitting at the table. She tried to say 'Katherine,' but her mouth was dry. No reply came in answer to the croaking sound she managed to make. She felt for her keys. They were still under the buttons of her bodice. She felt numb with cold and she found it hard to move her head. Frightened she put both hands up and felt the smooth ropes of hair to be tight and rigid. She knew at once they were wound, in and out, round the struts of the chair back. Cautiously she felt the chair lower down. Her hair was wound round and through and round and through. She was tied by her hair. Terrified by the knowledge of silent and sinister action she tried to get up from the chair but could not.

'Katherine!' she said in a crackling whisper. There was no reply. She tried again to call out. She had no voice for a cry or a scream. 'Kathy!' she tried once more.

She woke with a start. With a timid movement she put her hands to her head and to the chair back and knew she was free. Katherine, at the other side of the table, raised her head and blinked at her; then, gathering the rug about her, she moved from her chair to the old sofa. She lay down and pulled the rug round her shoulders and seemed to continue to sleep without really waking up.

Hester limped to the wood box. She would need to go out to the porch for more wood and kindling to relight the stove.

She thought she heard the voice as soon as she opened the door to the shining wet yard. It was still dark though the sky held, low down, the pale light of the approaching dawn. She listened and thought she heard the voice again. The poultry, not properly shut up, were making some commotion. She was not sure about the voice. Katherine had thrown, she said, the torch down the well. Hester had another little one which she fetched. She groped at the top edge of the wardrobe reminded by their fragrance of the ripeness and readiness of the quinces. The gun, she thought, used to be kept on the wardrobe but that was long ago in the other house. The gun, neglected, must be somewhere but would be useless. An intruder had come, a murderer perhaps, and she had no weapon.

With her weak torch she moved slowly across the yard. The air was fresh and cold and there was the sound of water everywhere. Her black polished boots splashed through a small lake. Water trickled and dripped from the gutters of the house and from the eaves of the shed. She thought, at first, that the voice called from the hay in the woolshed. The gun would not have been of any use. She knew it could easily be lost to an enemy for she did have the light in one hand and needed her stick in the other. She twisted her face in the bitter half smile. Perhaps it would be better not to go searching.

The voice, she was not sure now that she had heard anyone call, but the voice partly lost in the running and dripping of water seemed to come from the well. Unwillingly she went to the edge of the coping. There was water in the well. She could smell it. High water, terrifyingly high considering the depths. She turned the pale beam of her torch on the dark surging movement of the water, hardly able to follow the frail light with her look. She was afraid of the water and what its power might have yielded.

She knew how quickly flood water could rise. Bridges and paddocks could become impassable in less than ten minutes.

As her torch flashed again to the water making curious rings and rippling patterns of light on the black surface, she was sure she saw a hand grasping the lowest metal rung, the one which was set in the wall of the well at a greater distance below the other rungs. She thought as the water slapped crazily against the stonework that she saw too a man's head which, because of being drenched, was small, sleeked and rounded.

It is difficult to see anything which is partly and, at times, wholly submerged. Hester knew this as she tried to peer with her feeble light into the strangeness of the changed well. It seemed now that there was no sound other than the unusual sound of water coming from the well. And what she thought she had seen was now completely submerged. Peering, she waited for some sign. To her horror the water seemed to be rising even more. Soon, she thought, it would cover the next rung and then the next.

Hester knew that the quick rising of water was often followed by an equally quick fall of the raised level. Trembling and fearful at the thought of what was now so close to the edge of the coping, she raised her stick and tried to lean into the hole. Supporting herself on the wall she tried, with the slender ash plant, to poke at whatever it was just below the level of the water. Not able to reach she struck wildly and without effect with the stick. He must go down.

'Down!' she said in a voice which she did not know was her own. 'Go down!' Go on! Down! Go back down!'

Because of the lowest rung being so much further down and the gap between that rung and the next one up being so much greater, anyone hanging on by one hand there could not possibly reach up to the next one unless lifted by something; a tremendous upward surge of water perhaps. The hand reaching the next rung would enable the other hand to move to the rung above that. She did not want to consider the possibilities and she was not able to reach down far enough to bring about any change. If only she could find the hand and the head and then, reaching them, get rid of them for ever. 'Down! Go back down!' She bit her lip till it bled, knowing with a hardly suppressed anger that the man, if he was there, was not anything more than a corpse. Helplessness and anger made her weak.

Suddenly the enormity of what she was trying to do made her stop.

If she turned the Toyota and backed up close to the well she could simply pay out enough rope after fixing it firmly. She began to wonder in a confused and desperate way where to fix the end of the rope. All her sense could not have deserted her.

Turning the truck was simple. The sound of the engine starting and the rasping of the wet gravel was like her father's car turning in the night, years ago, when Hilde cried. That night when Hilde cried so much, blood-stained and frightened, in the candlelit bathroom.

Quickly it had become all to clear. The petted, nimble and courageous little crippled girl grew into a tall clumsy adolescent female. The father who had once hoped with what he knew to be his only chance for a son must have hoped again for a son, a healthy capable boy, a partner and a companion, without bargaining with the attitudes of his mother, Hester's grandmother, and not knowing fully her punishments. His shame and disappointment must have accompanied him through all the years as did the memory of the banishing of Hilde Herzfeld accompany Hester herself, having turned away – as she did then, not wanting to know – from the terrible and secret pain.

Not all that for Katherine. None of it for Kathy. How could she, Hester, Miss Harper dear, have ever considered it. How could she have suggested to Kathy that she make herself pretty and go down for what was cowshed and corner-of-the-paddock business. The mating of cattle for stock was all right for the beasts and for some people but it was not for Kathy. Not for her dainty innocence.

She did not want to bring this man out of the well. She had a very good reason for putting him there in the first place. To contradict one's own actions was, to say the least, a waste of valuable energy.

How would it be possible, she wondered, to hitch the rope under the sodden armpits of the man. She supposed that somehow it could be done. Against her own will she turned the sturdy little truck again and backed it right up to the stone coping. She tried to move quickly but knew that she was slow. The coil of rope on the floor of the cabin was strong and real. In her hands she felt it was powerful. Again and again as she felt the rope she wondered at its strength and at its clumsiness. It would be impossible to fix the rope to anything. She peered in the darkness as if a miraculous post could appear firmly in the paved part of the yard. She stood back from the truck, undecided, holding her fading torch so that she could see the dark, partly uncoiled, loops of rope. The well water gurgled and splashed slapping as it was forced upwards from below. She could imagine the holes in the rocks far down through which the water was making its way, trickling slowly in places and then gushing to fill caverns. As more water flowed underground and the small openings and channels became blocked with earth and stones, more water would be forced upwards in the wide shaft of the well. Perhaps the paths of the invisible streams were partially blocked by the pieces of china she had so light-heartedly tossed away.

Somewhere in that surging water was her money. Money weathered water. Perhaps it would surface wrinkled and encrusted on the desolate edges of the salt lakes, those ugly places, unvisited, somewhere further on, far off and lower down beyond the end of the track. Places where Hester had never wanted to go.

She could just make out in the distance over the far brow of the paddock two large yellow eyes. Two subdued tawny lights advancing slowly. Hester recognized them as tractor lights. She could hear the low pitch of the steady reliable engine and she knew how well the wheels would, in their strength, eat away the distance, however impassable the ground was for an ordinary car or truck. She wondered why anyone would be out at this time of night. She thought it must be Mr Borden.

'He must be mad!' she said to herself fondling the thick rope, turning it over in her usually capable hands, knowing that any farmer would be out as soon as he could after the storm to see as quickly as possible the damage, and to see what needed doing and in what order . . .

The rope suggesting rescue as she uncoiled more of it made her consider the man's place in the house. There was a spare bed, the one prepared for Joanna. It was in Kathy's room. That would not do. But that was what they would want. A small shudder went through her. They would close the door . . .

The idea of Kathy bearing a child could not be thought

about and the idea of some man, that man, touching or handling her perfectly made and childlike body was repulsive. The man would make demands. He would want Kathy's time and she, Hester, was no longer of an age to be sent to bed leaving the long evenings free for other people. Kathy would be completely absorbed by him. She would want to look after him, to cherish him. Hester thought of the new pretty curtains and the bed coverlet prepared for the other unwanted guest. She bent down, groaning, to see if the rope could in some way be wound round some part of the body of the Toyota. Perhaps the three of them – Joanna and the man who said to call him Jacob and Kathy – would want to live in the house. 'Miss Harper, dear,' she could hear the purring voice, 'we have found the darlingest rest-home for yew – in town – yes we'll be able to visit yew, Miss Harper, dear . . .'

The rope began to fall in heavy unwieldy curves, it was getting wet.

The throbbing of the tractor engine seemed to be a part of a nightmare, yet she was not asleep. She wondered if she was ill. She could not bring herself to look again into the darkness of the well. The morning was coming quickly, all the familiar buildings and the stunted trees of the small orchard were taking shape. She longed to hear the usual singing sound of emptiness, the wind moaning and the faint, partly imagined suggestion of water somewhere a long way down the well.

The tractor was alongside the wire fence. She thought of the white hand, knuckles scraped bare to the bone, grasping the rung, and of the head soaked and vulnerable . . . She felt herself trembling.

'How you making out over there Miss Harper?' a voice called out. Looking up Hester saw young Mr Borden leap from the tractor. Hester straightened up letting the rope lie in the wet.

'What a night of it, Miss Harper!' Mr Borden called from the fence. 'Thought I'd creep over to see how you're making out. Everything okay?'

'We seem to be fine thank you, Mr Borden,' Hester called back, surprised at herself. 'I hope all's well at your end,' she forced herself to be as gracious as she could. She had not come home, at sixteen, from boarding school, in the middle of a term, to keep house for her father, her grandmother having died suddenly, and not learned how to speak to the men.

'Big wash away!' he called. 'Lot of damage can't size it up all at once.'

'No,' Hester said. 'I'm sorry,' she added.

'Anything there you need help with?' Mr Borden stepped, with powerful thighs, over the wires. Hester noticed with approval that he did not press them down, his long legs cleared them beautifully.

'Well cover's slipped has it?' he said crossing the yard.

'It's been like that for years now,' Hester began.

'No worries.' Mr Borden bent down and dragged, it seemed without effort, the well cover into its proper position.

'It's very old,' Hester said, staring at the ragged hole and tapping the exposed timber with her stick.

'How about I send someone over,' Mr Borden said breaking off a small piece of rusted iron, 'patch this up in no time.' He tossed the rusty fragment into the hole.

'If you can spare a man . . .' Hester said.

'No worries,' Mr Borden said, 'I'll send over later today.'

'I'd like it closed over completely,' Hester said, 'and fixed all the way round'

'Will do,' Mr Borden said. He stepped back over the fence and waved his hand as he climbed back on to the tractor.

Hester gave a small wave, the smallest wave one person can give to another . . .

'Goose,' Mrs Grossman, wonderfully florid with conversation, was saying, 'if I at this very minute was to cook a goose for Mr Grossman's tea I am not a liar if he'd sooner be dead.'

The shop was crowded. The town's new creative population and the more recent landowners (small parcels mainly) were fetching cartons of skimmed milk and selecting wrapped sliced bread. Mrs Grossman, enjoying her audience, drew breath to enlarge on what happened inside Mr Grossman when he ate a goose.

The reverend doctor, studying detergents as if for a postgraduate thesis, moved aside hardly nodding to Hester as she sat down on one of the bentwood chairs. She, as before, envied his ability to concentrate. It was some years since they had exchanged greetings. She wondered what his subjects of conversation were now, wondering too if she would have anything to offer if he did speak to her.

'And another thing! Just take a look willya at them exotic dancers. I'll give them Fur and Feathers!' Snorting, Mrs Grossman moved on to other subjects on which she enjoyed holding opinions.

'But *my deah!* Such *beautiful* bards, one simply cannot *eat* them! They are so *intelligent* too!'

'Excuse me!' Mrs Grossman accused some slices of ham

before folding them in grease-proof paper. 'People do, but,' she said, 'I know a woman – couldn't set eyes on a goose but she'd have to cook it. My own mother, believe you me, was the same. Show her a goose and she'd have its neck broke before you could say "knife". . .'

Hester, perched stiffly on the uncomfortable little chair, waited for Mr Grossman to finish putting up her groceries. For a few moments Miss Harper was customer number one; Mrs Borden had not yet appeared. Hester was reflecting on this good fortune when another customer, entering the shop, took the other bentwood chair. 'Mind if I take a pew?' Hester recognized the woman whose quest a few days earlier had been a square bowl, plastic but square for feet. 'I'm working on a book, that's why we bought a little property out here, to get away, as they say, from it all.'

'Yes,' Hester said, 'you told me about your poem last time.'

'Did I?' the writer said, her eyes keen. 'I think it's going to be an epic,' she said. 'A sort of contemporary *Song of Solomon.*'

'I see,' Hester said. She was suddenly overcome with hunger. Unable to battle with the pangs she selected a lamington roll from the edge of the counter. Tearing off its clear wrapper she ate the whole cake enjoying every large mouthful and letting the white shreds of coconut litter her black bodice.

The other woman watched with admiration. 'I say,' she said, 'do you often do that?'

Hester, with her mouth too full, nodded.

'Sort of eat now and pay later.'

Hester nodded again.

'D'you think that I -?

Hester swallowed. 'Of course,' she said. Quickly the woman, without hesitating in her choice, took a chocolate swiss roll and with a skill nearly as great as Hester's demolished it. 'To get back to my book,' she said licking her fingers, 'I'm writing a perfectly horrific little drama set, do you see, in a remote corner of the wheat. Very regional. It's strictly a novella. In writing it I have to keep to certain rules which have been accepted in literary circles. I'm in trouble already . . .'

'Oh?' Hester tried to look concerned.

'Yes, the tradition is that the story has a narrator who has gone through all the experiences in the novella and is relating them. I simply have no narrator!' She sighed.

'Oh what a shame!' Hester was not accustomed to being at a complete loss for words.

'Yes, the novella has to be a narrative, fiction of course, longer than a short story but can be quite short for all that.'

'I see,' Hester said again.

'The characters can have names but they are mainly known by what they do in life – in their everyday life . . .'

'Like,' Hester was inspired, 'the butcher, the baker, the candlestick maker . . .'

'Yes, that's the sort of thing and we do have such a wide canvas here in town, the potter, the painter, the carpenter, the shopkeeper, the landowner, the orphan, the stock and station agent and the intruder. As a novelist,' the new acquaintance continued, 'I need an intruder to distort a relationship. The action goes forward but is governed by the events of everyday life. Perhaps using the seasons as a kind of hinge of fate and with an understanding of events being inevitable because that's what life's all about isn't it –– the rich dark fruit cake of life.' She sighed again.

'You mean,' Hester said, becoming interested in spite of herself, 'that people go on making the best of things.''

'It's not quite so simple, not so simple in fiction . . .'

'It's not simple in ordinary life surely,' Hester said.

'That's so,' her temporary companion on the other chair said. 'I am looking for a narrator with experiences.' She snatched off her spectacles and, putting her face close, she peered through her long hair at Hester. 'The novella,' she continued, 'could contain too a detailed, a fairly detailed, description of a contemporary illness, anorexia nervosa for example, and there's always herpes and AIDS to fall back on. There are certain things people like to read about, you know, misfortunes, conflicts, passions and emotions – all rather heightened . . . I'd also put in . . .'

'Miss Harper's order coming up!' Mr Grossman, staggering on bent legs, came round the open end of the counter. 'Under the tarp? As usual Miss Harper?'

'Yes please,' Hester struggled to her feet grasping her stick. Hesitating she nodded to her new friend and followed Mr Grossman out into the street where the freshly washed Toyota was parked.

'We could have – us both, Mr Grossman and I, been raped and worse in our beds.' Mrs Grossman's voice followed them. Theft and double rape was the next item it seemed. 'Three tyarias gorn from Bordens. Mrs Borden will never see them again that's for sure. My own dyamontey tyaria too!' Mrs Grossman, in the short interval of time had evidently amassed a jewelry collection of her own. One of the gifts of theft. A legacy from a thief. A tiara for Mrs Grossman. If she had had it in time, Hester thought without meaning to think, Mrs Grossman could have worn her tiara at her wedding.

Hester and Katherine, redolent of a particularly powerful tar shampoo left over from the days when Hester, regularly on Sundays, furiously lathered her father's ancient dogs, drove on down the High Street to the post office. Their joint hair washing had been the final act of a merciless cleaning programme in readiness for the coming of Joanna and, in part, as a sort of celebration of the closing of the well.

Mr Borden, as good as his word, had sent two men and the necessary materials soon after daybreak. Hester saw them arrive as if from outer space across the great distance of the paddock. In the silent kitchen she, as quietly as possible, prepared a breakfast which she ate with a good appetite. Approaching the sofa she gently shook Katherine saying, 'Kathy wake up! Everything's cleared up in the yard. The men have practically finished. Wash your face! I'm calling the men in for tea and scones. I've baked scones, Kathy, time to get up.'

Katherine, puffy about the eyes, drank her hot tea and tossed her tangled hair in reply to some joking remark from one of the men. The rain brought out jokes from the men Hester remembered. It brought out bold remarks too.

'You, Kathy, you coming to the dancing?' one of the men, the older one, asked. 'There's dancing at the fête next week. There's disco and a barn dance. I saw you at Borden's show, you like the dancing? eh?' He whistled a tune through his teeth and moved his shoulders, first one and then the other. He tapped his foot on the kitchen tiles making muddy marks Hester noticed. Katherine pouted and narrowed her eyes. She squinted at him sideways and tossed her hair again.

'Katherine has a friend coming to stay,' Hester said.

'Great! See you both there!' He scraped his chair back from the table. 'Thanks for the tea Miss Harper.' He put his cup on the draining board. The younger man, following, muttered his thanks adding a mumbled, 'See ya at the dance then,' to Katherine.

During those few days, during the relentless cleaning of the rooms, the relining of the scrubbed-out cupboards with fresh shelf paper, the airing of more blankets and the sewing of yet another frilled quilt for Joanna's bed, Hester was sure Mr Bird would come. She looked frequently across the paddocks to the rise to watch for his cloud of dust and then remembered, as if stepping into another world, that the rain had come and there would be no dust. The steady drone of the tractors, sometimes near and sometimes far off, as they crossed and recrossed ploughing the rain-softened earth, enhanced the emptiness and the isolation.

But Mr Bird did not come. Hester dressed two ducks and a boiling fowl. Though their immediate pantry needed restocking they had a good cupboard of their own pre-serves. Hester opened bottled carrots, beans and tomatoes and, as a special treat, she brought out a vintage cherry jam made by her grandmother. Together they dug over their

159 ☆

own vegetable plots using their light forks. Hester, leaning on her fork, declared the ground ready after the rain. She was, she said, obliged to do more leaning than digging.

The two women sat in the Toyota outside the post office to look at their letters. Hester's were all requests for money for worthwhile, she hoped, charities and relief organizations. Katherine had a letter on blue pages with scalloped edges. Every page was decorated with a golden cross, the scallops were also gilded. The general effect was pretty.

'It's from Joanna,' Katherine said when Hester questioned.

Katherine had developed a different way of speaking. Her voice was flat and often she did not look up when she replied to anything Hester said.

Hester understood that Katherine was tired. She tried, a few times, to reason with her that the well was completely covered – hadn't she seen for herself? – the men finishing off all that needed doing when she, Hester, had told her breakfast was ready. Hester, at the back of her mind, wondered whether it was possible to really close off the incident in this simple way. If she brought it all into normal circumstances (two men working at the well, repairing the cover, when Katherine unravelled herself from the tartan rug) then Katherine had no tale to tell, nothing to blurt out, because Hester had to believe that Katherine would believe that the two men working so diligently would know by now all there was to know. So, Hester said to herself, what had Kathy to tell? It seemed all so simple. She hoped it was the end of the horrible affair. All she had to do now was to suppress, to squash her own miserable knowledge, pull her bedclothes over her head as she had on the night of Hilde's pain, and get through, first the visit from Joanna and then whatever was to come after that.

She would concentrate on the jam and pickle shed. This would keep them busy. They could start with the quinces. The fruit would keep for a few more days. Making quince jelly would probably be a new experience for Joanna.

Hester tried to look forward to the pretty little jars glowing in neat rows on the kitchen table.

'Joanna's just sent me her train arrival time which we know already,' Katherine replied. Hester listened anxiously for some kind of change in her voice

'Is that all?' Hester peered across at the pages. 'There's more than that surely.' Katherine seemed to read the rest of the letter as if she had not read it just before. 'She, Joanna's into religion,' she said, her voice beginning to lift. 'She's an evangelist. Oh, Miss Harper, dear,' she said with more life, 'she wants me to be an evangelist too. Isn't that cute? There's a college in America . . . where . . .'

Hester, scanning the pages quickly, saw the glittering crosses, like Christmas decorations, on the pages and the tiny gold writing, very curved and ornamental, a text, above the heavy rounded handwriting of the future visitor.

> *See!*
> *I will not forget you . . .*
> *I have carved you on the palm of my hand*

She supposed it was the same text on every page.

'Oh yes,' Katherine said, 'it would cost too much, wouldn't it, to have writing paper with different things on every page. Evangelist!' she said. 'Isn't that just Great! America! Great!'

I'll drop you outside the markets,' Hester said pulling to the side of the road. 'You can buy a new pillow for the spare bed and have a little look round. I'll be back here in half an hour or so when I've been to see Mr Bird. See if there's something you fancy, something you fancy to eat this evening,' she added, knowing that she was, against her principles, pandering to a sudden capriciousness in Katherine's appetite. She had eaten hardly anything during the last few days since the well had been sealed with the repaired cover. Diligently she had prepared everything as usual, taking great trouble with the preserved vegetables and fruit and, serving for them both the usual attractive helpings and then, without any explanation or apology, had either refused or been unable to eat. Hester trying to be calm felt an overwhelming tenderness for Kathy as she drove away seeing her in the rear mirror white faced and delicate at the entrance to the busy market. She would have liked to hold her close to say comforting words but she was afraid to break the calm and she was not sure what words to say. Kathy had mentioned a college. There was Joanna and the college. She could not think of Kathy going away, not just yet. Not yet. Not ever.

Mr Bird's house which was also his office had a piece of rough lawn surrounded by a cyclone wire fence with white painted posts and rails. It was set back from the road, the shaggy grass patch sloping up to the house. At the back of the house was a stockfeeder's barn and a loading ramp. As she drove into the yard Hester saw that the barn was closed.

There were no trees or flowers though a passion vine still clung to a trellis which hid, Hester remembered suddenly, a shed and an outside lavatory. It was a long time since she had visited Mr Bird. Everything looked the same in spite of the passing of years. The only difference was that no one was about. Nothing was being loaded or unloaded, the barn looked strange with its usually gaping doorway closed.

There were never any children at Mr Bird's house when she went there as a child with her father. But there had been, all by itself in an accessible corner of the shed, an old wooden dolls' pram. It was handmade and heavy and had not been painted. It had round wooden wheels and when Hester pulled it out from the shed and pushed it on Mr Bird's path it had rumbled and bumped along as she imagined a prehistoric pram would have done – if prehistoric people had had prams. Hester pushed the pram up and down the path while her father discussed things with Mr Bird.

It was disturbing now to remember the pram, the only toy at Mr Bird's place. She had never wondered till now how he came to have something that could be played with. She wondered now if he had made it himself and, if so, why. Perhaps today she would ask him and perhaps even thank him for sending her cards for both birthdays at school. She would thank quietly, of course, for she had to speak to him today very carefully. She must ask him to help her to rearrange her investments as she needed money. She had to consider and decide on the best way of talking about this as she naturally could not disclose to him the terrible loss. She had to endure that second to the other thing she must endure on her own. She must never speak about either.

The wooden pram did not have any covers or any pillow and once when Hester put her doll, brought on purpose to have an outing in Mr Bird's pram, into the pram it had slipped down into the deep well of the pram in a most awkward way. Hester tried to rescue the doll but it was wedged somehow. She poked at the small round head of the doll marking and scratching, without meaning to, the sleek shining paint which the doll had for hair. Not wanting to tell anyone, she had pushed the pram back into the shed upset by the offended and hurt look the doll seemed to have on its red-cheeked face. Neither her father nor Mr Bird noticed the emptiness in Hester's arms when it was time to leave.

Mr Bird's small house was extremely plain and dull Hester thought as she limped round the side. She had always imagined it to be filled with filing cabinets and spikes packed with yellowing papers, bills and receipts and records of sales and purchases long forgotten. She knew that there were people who could never throw away such papers. She needed some tea and wondered if Mr Bird, after her last churlish behaviour, would offer her some. She supposed he could make tea somewhere in his house. He might even have a tin of biscuits. She could not remember ever having anything to eat there. He must have some meals, she thought, that were not in other people's houses.

It was so quiet Hester had to realize that Mr Bird was not at home. She should have known he would be out, away visiting properties and sales. She was so out of touch she did not know what would be going on at present. It was strange too that the stock-feed barn was closed.

The office door was open. There was a girl in the small room bent over a pile of envelopes, sorting them.

'I suppose Mr Bird is out.' Hester broke into the silence, at the same time remembering the small-scale yards at the forthcoming fête. Mostly the show was for domestic and farm-yard animals and poultry. There would even be a section for children's pets. Mr Bird, thin and distinguished looking in tweeds and his best hat, would be at every suitable elbow his eyes narrowing towards the flanks of some innocent sow.

'Yes he is.' The young woman looked up. 'Is there anything I can do for you Miss Harper?'

'When will he be back?' Hester was annoyed and worried.

'I don't know.' The woman, Hester saw now when she got up from behind the tidy desk, was not young, only her face was youthful. Hester recognized her as the wife of the man who worked in the stock-feed barn. The office was airless and very neat. 'He's had to go to hospital,' she said, 'not here in town. He's been taken away to the city. Frank went with him. He was taken ill during the night . . . they might be able to do an operation . . . The office,' she smiled at Hester, 'is really closed but if there's anything . . . I can get fowl pellets if that's . . .'

Hester, leaning on her stick, swayed and sat down on one of the wooden chairs placed along the wall. She had never considered the possibility that something might happen to Mr Bird. She felt as if she was on the edge of a black hole. She, in spite of a great fear and dread, managed to utter something which bordered on a sound of sympathy and, no, it was not layer pellets she wanted.

'We don't know what's wrong exactly,' Frank's wife said, 'but it wasn't altogether sudden, he's had some bad spells and then apparently a big haemorrhage, internal – you see, he's alone here at night. Frank,' she indicated with a jerk of her head, the barn, 'Frank found him first thing in the morning. They wouldn't keep him at the hospital here – said he must go at once . . . he'd had a few bad spells, Frank knew that, but we didn't know how bad.' She paused. 'Is it your books you want to see Miss Harper?' she asked. 'They are all here if you want them. Mr Bird keeps everything so people can see what's what. He has them locked in here. I can get them for you . . . He's got everyone's affairs safe in here.'

'Thank you,' Hester said and waited and was handed, in a few moments, the little pile of cheap exercise books.

I'll get you a cup of tea while you have a read,' Frank's wife said. 'The kettle won't take a minute. I expect you could do with one.'

'Thank you.' Hester forced her voice to be gracious. She opened the red exercise book which was filled from cover to cover with Mr Bird's surprisingly neat figures and handwriting. In this book, with carefully entered dates, were all the investments neatly listed under headings underlined with red ink. ***HOLDER STOCK AMOUNT INTEREST PURCHASED MATURING INTEREST DUE RECEIVED CERTIFICATE NUMBER*** There were the lists of figures spreading across the pages tirelessly written out year after year.

In another book the details of the land and house and crop sales were listed, everything was there, all the terms of the transaction down to the last teaspoon sold in the contents of the house.

In the yellow exercise book she read:

At present all investments are in one of three groups. Inscribed stock is recorded in a central register. In the case of inscribed stock it is not essential to have the original certificates though it is useful to have a record. The Savings Bonds can be cashed at one month's notice and the Central Authority Bonds can be cashed on application to the treasury. If cashed before maturity the money received may be less than nominal value. The maturity dates of the various Bonds are recorded in the red book. Usually when a loan matures an opportunity is given to convert to a new loan . . .

Hester blinked and made herself read on.

As the value of money declines steadily it would be desirable but may not be possible to put some further money aside each year.

Information about new Bonds, Miss Hester, is advertised in the paper and a prospectus will usually be sent to the holder of stock.

Debentures: These are also Fixed Interest Securities for a specific period. They do not have Government backing but the ones held should be safe. With Debentures it is necessary to preserve carefully, Miss Hester, the stock certificate and these are lodged and held at the Bank.

Cash Management Trust: The money in cash management trust is available at twenty four hours notice. The Capital ought to be secure but the interest fluctuates according to variations in the money market. There is no fixed term for the investment. It is necessary to have some money readily available for unexpected or large expenses . . .

Hester was hardly able to read on, her eyes were blurred with tears. It was the second time within a few days that her eyes had been washed like this.

The tea cup inscribed with the words *Shire Roads Board* stood on the edge of the desk. She tried to read on.

Property and other Trusts. In addition to the investments already listed there are now investments which are intended to produce capital gains and either give no interest or very little . . . none of these investments should be given up before at least three years if possible . . . there is a fee charged . . .

Hester had to wipe her eyes. She kept her head bent down.

These investments at the time of writing are, Miss Hester . . .

She could not go on reading. The little exercise books were a powerful indication of how she had been looked after and she was ashamed because she had never wanted to know and had never given a glance or a smile of gratitude or a word of thanks. She understood too, at once, that she needed to be looked after, cared for, more than ever. She had never felt so afraid and so alone.

'Have a chocolate-chip biscuit Miss Harper and have your tea before it's cold.' Mrs Frank's voice came, it seemed, across a great space.

'Yes, yes, thank you.' Hester felt the thick old cup with her lips and tried to drink. It was an ugly cup but the tea was nice.

'If you want to leave your instructions Miss Harper,' Mrs Frank said, 'I'll be happy to see to anything as you want done.'

'When will Mr Bird be back?' Hester had no idea what her instructions should be. 'I'll need his advice,' she was going to add but did not.

'That I can't say at all,' Mrs Frank said, 'but I daresay it'd be all right for you to take the books to go over at your leisure and be sure to bring them back to the office next time you're in town – them being the only records. Should you want cash you can go to the bank and ask for Mr Taylor. Mr Bird said to tell you that if you . . .'

'I see,' Hester struggled to her feet. 'Thank you,' she said, putting the thin books in her handbag. She was afraid more tears would come and be in evidence on her cheeks. Not for the first time in her life someone, another person, had left some words of advice, of help, for her. Perhaps, like last time, she would never be able to tell the person, the friend, thank you. It was the pain of bereavement. 'I'll be back in town in a couple of days,' she managed to say. 'We'll be coming in to meet the train.'

'Oh well, I'll see you then, then,' Mrs Frank said, 'and by

then we should know for better or for worse how it's to be for poor Mr Bird.'

'Yes,' Hester said. She limped away down the path to the Toyota. Katherine would be waiting.

Hester is walking at the side of the long straight road low down between the brown paddocks which stretch endlessly on both sides to far-away horizons. A practical consideration which can bring a human being into perspective, she thinks, is the knowledge that a tiny handful of people can produce from this vast landscape enormous quantities of food. The great dome of the familiar sky is above like a never-ending floating roof of light clear air. Once again there are no clouds though her keen eyes do detect, she thinks, a faint blur which could be cloud perhaps even rain-bearing cloud. It is at present far away. It seems to lie, hardly suspended, above the place where the land meets the sky.

She carries a petrol can in one hand. With the other hand she leans heavily on her stick and, in spite of the built-up surgical boot and the iron caliper, she is limping along at quite a good pace. Never in all her years of driving to and from the town or to other properties has she run out of petrol. It is not her way to be unprepared. She does know though, from experience, that the deserted road only seems to be deserted. It is a curious fact about driving in the country that other cars on the road are kept spaced by distance because they are all travelling at about the same speed. The driver forced to stop for one reason or another, thinking that he is alone in the most remote and forlorn place, soon finds that he is overtaken by one car after another. And, in the country, it is the habit for drivers to slow down and stop and ask if there is anything they can do. Even for their sworn enemies they will do this.

As she walks she tells herself that she must enjoy the feeling of her own insignificance which is enhanced by the indifference of the land. This silent indifference towards human life can make her feel small and safe. It is a safety which brings freedom for the time being. It is a freedom from fear. As she is able to sift her thoughts and feelings she knows, as she has always known, if there are several fears then there are really none. One fear on its own, is really fear and it is one fear that she has. Out between the apparently deserted paddocks it seems to be dissipated and she can say aloud in a croaking sort of voice, talking to herself, that if Kathy wants to go with Joanna to the city – to America – wherever it is people go these days, she, Hester, must not mind. Of course she minds, she says; she does mind . . . The text on Joanna's pretty blue paper must be an American version of

> *yet will I not forget thee.*
> *Behold I have graven thee*
> *upon the palms of my hands;*

Hester has looked it up in her Bible. She, when she did this, was wanting to tell Katherine that America was not all film stars and beautiful houses in Beverley Hills. Katherine was serving their evening meal. Her appetite had come back and Hester, remembering a dreadfully sad story they had read together in a magazine, did not say anything. In the story which was said to be a true story, a young girl, caught in an emotional conflict, refused to eat and then was unable to eat and came to a terrible end.

Kathy reduced to a skeleton sitting on the edge of a hospital bed. Never!

Hester knows that her thoughts at a certain time every

morning are like recurring symptoms. These thoughts come in waves each one adding to the one before, like the waves of an illness. Her mind is swamped every morning while the breakfast is cleared away and the kitchen floor is swept and washed. She feels the obsession coming over her and she can think only of Kathy, of her appearance, of the sound of her voice, and of her dancing. She thinks of how Kathy will tell her that she wants to go away and leave her and she thinks of what she must say in reply and she wants to break down and weep before this conversation can take place. She wants to beg her not to go, not to want to go. During this time of obsession she cannot face a life without Kathy; every day to wake up and know that she is no longer there. She does not speak of it, however, because of the delicate balance of reason which can so easily be disturbed. In her mind, at these times, she goes over the words and phrases, over and over the same thoughts and the same words and the same phrases . . .

And now as she walks she can think of these daily overwhelming thoughts and she knows they come as an expected pain comes and they go as a pain, going, goes.

It is simply a matter she tells herself of not thinking and a matter of keeping thoughts and wishes in proportion. . . and it is a matter of resolving not to go over endlessly unspoken conversations. If Kathy does go away. If she has to face this it will be a matter of having enough activities to partially disguise the emptiness.

Katherine is left behind, perched high in the Toyota. Hester was just able, as they came to an unexpected halt, to pull off onto the gravel. The shoulder of the road being on the crest of a slight rise there was the land spread out all round them. Possibilities in all directions Hester said but the wisest choice was to wait with the truck or to start walking, with the can, along the road towards *El Bandito*.

As Hester felt like walking they decided that Katherine should remain there and finish the hand-sewing on the Rosalind costume, a lovely woodland green, Hester having found among her store of materials a suitable length of cloth. It would have been pointless, they both agreed, to cut out the doublet for Orlando (purple) until Joanna was measured for as, Hester said at the time in a way in which Hilde Herzfeld might have said it, Joanna might turn out to be a dumpling. Also, Kathy had another thought, it would be better not to dye the pantihose until Joanna said if she liked purple. Getting Rosalind finished would leave enough time to sew Orlando before the day of the jam and pickle shed.

There is plenty of time for a breakdown before they meet the train which is bringing Joanna. They left early so that Hester would have time to visit Mr Bird's house again, the idea being that Katherine would finish the sewing at the station while waiting for the train to come.

Hester is just remembering the cassette, 'Buttoned up Beats', which she bought at *El Bandito* on the day of the rope and which she forgot to give to Katherine when Mrs Rosalie Borden with her diesel land cruiser packed with small, well-scrubbed boys overtakes her. She has already, coming upon the stranded Toyota, spoken to Katherine.

'No worries, Miss Harper,' Mrs Borden calls out, 'move up over boys – into the back and let Miss Harper into the front. That's it Dobby, take the drum for Miss Harper. Not like you at all, Miss Harper to run out of gas!'

'No,' Hester says, trying with difficulty to heave herself up into the front seat. 'No it's never happened to me before.'

'One of youse take Miss Harper's stick.' Rosalie Borden's rich tones of command are obeyed instantly. Hester notices that she is only just able to fit behind the steering wheel.

'Junior here,' Mrs Borden pats her almost full-term bulge with affection, 'drives. We'll get you there and back in no time.'

'Miss Harper,' Dobby Borden says, 'your spotlight on your roo bar's broke.'

Broken, Hester says in her mind. 'Is it?' she says twisting to look at the child.

'Yes, under the cover it's all splintery', his piping voice fills the car, 'all smashed and splintery . . .'

'Manners! Dobby Borden. Voice! Dobby Borden for gawd's sake! Keep that voice of yours down,' Mrs Rosalie Borden, apparently unaware of her own powerful sounds, admonishes. 'Miss Harper's not deaf. She's got ears like everyone else!'

'I suppose I must have . . .' Hester fumbles for words. 'I must . . .'

'Did you get a roo? Did you Miss Harper? Did you get a roo?' The children's excited noisy voice seem all round her.

'Boys! Manners! Shut up the lot of you!' Rosalie Borden quietens her sons. 'I expect,' she says, 'Miss Harper's had dozens of roos on that great big bar in her time. Tell you what. She'll get one of you if you don't keep quiet! She'll get all of youses, that's what.'

'Oh no, no, I don't think I . . .' Hester starts to speak.

'Aw! it's only my fun,' Mrs Borden says, 'they know!' In the ensuing silence Mrs Borden, in an amiable and relaxed way, begins to gossip about Mr Bird's sudden illness and death. 'An aortic haemorrhage they said it was,' she says. 'They say the end's quick but nothing is really all that quick; there's always what there is when anyone dies.' She keeps her hands lightly on the steering wheel which does seem to be held firmly by her pregnancy. 'I knew he'd been unwell for quite a while,' she adds.

'Yes,' Hester manages to say. She finds it hard to breathe easily and the car movement makes her feel sick. Mrs Borden is still talking, telling her that Mr Borden's younger brother who is a distributor, – 'distributes anything and everything,' Mrs Borden laughs, 'got his fingers in everywhere, frozen foods, soft ware, ladies' underwear, pantihose and corsets. Books puts books in all the stores, cassettes, records – you name it – he carries it – is interested in Mr Bird's business. Mr Borden,' Mrs Borden continues, 'says his brother will bring the agency up to date with computers and everything. Did you know, Miss Harper,' Rosalie Borden's voice is filled with curiosity and disbelief, 'did you know, Miss Harper, that Old Birdie wrote out every sum and every word all by hand!'

'I know,' Hester says and for the first time she thinks about the pain Mr Bird must have endured. And how, like Hilde, bloodstained and in pain, he must have thought about her and the things that would worry her and, hardly able to speak, he had left some words for her.

'All ready with the jams and pickles Katherine was telling me,' Mrs Borden is saying. 'We had quite a nice little chat about this and that. The herring-bone stitching on her sewing is very nicely done, very firm and even – I didn't think anyone did herring-bone these days.' As Hester makes no reply Mrs Borden changes the subject. 'The fête should be good this year,' she says. 'We've a great many newcomers to the town, brings business and money. I think we'll raise enough for the town pool we're hoping to have, don't you think so Miss Harper?'

'Oh yes,' Hester manages to say. A town fête she thinks to herself, can provide money and money can do things to alleviate and ameliorate as people, doing all the things they do, move through life. Like moving a wood heap, log by log, to alter some detail of living. All the same, her thoughts continue, people have to endure. She also must endure.

'Tell us about the roos you got Miss Harper.' Dobby Borden, unable to keep silence any longer, is spokesman for the restless little boys.

'If you're very quiet and manage to sit quite still for the next three minutes till we get to the roadhouse,' Rosalie Borden says, 'on the way back with the gas Miss Harper will tell you all about a Great – Big – Monster she caught on her roo bar One Dark Night!' She gives a rich laugh and dropping her voice, speaking out of the corner of her mouth, she says, 'I said – "on the way back" – Miss Harper, to give you time to think up something.'

Hester is suddenly afraid. Afraid that Katherine will have blurted out something to Mrs Borden. She has not tried to extract from Katherine a promise of silence. She has simply said that the whole thing was over and cleared away and closed off and that there was no need to discuss any aspect of it ever again. Katherine's only reply was a quiet and dutiful, 'Yes, Miss Harper,' a reply which came, Hester thought at the time, as if straight from the orphanage.

'Oh dear,' Hester manages a forced little laugh. 'I really know nothing about children. I am not used to telling stories to children.' As a passenger in the car, possibly an unwelcome one, she thinks, as Mrs Borden is always sure to be in a terrible hurry to get done all she has to get done, she ought to be able to amuse the children for a few minutes. Mrs Borden has plenty to do without going back and forth on the road just for her.

'Miss Harper! Miss Harper! Make it real scarey!' Dobby Borden yells through the gaps in his teeth.

What was it the woman on the other chair in Grossman's said about the story having to be a narrative fiction told by someone who has actually had the experience. Hester draws her lips together in one of her half smiles, the smallest smile a person can give.

'I'll try and think. I'll have to decide which monster I'll tell you about,' she says.

'Miss Harper, real scarey! Make it real scarey!'

'Yes, Miss Harper, do that,' Rosalie Borden, spitting on one finger, smoothes her eye brows first one and then the other, approving of herself in the small reflection in the rear mirror. 'Scare 'em witless. They'll love it!'

As they drive back with the petrol they can see the gun-metal colour of the Toyota gleaming on the slight rise. The immense landscape dwarfs all human life. Hester is grateful for the smallness of the Toyota. It is not possible from this distance to see the small figure within bent with devotion over her sewing. In a few years Hester thinks they will all be gone, even these children, *as the one dieth, so dieth the other.* Of course she cannot say this aloud and these children are so much alive, their life seems to come through their skin.

'It was one dark night,' she tells them, 'along this very road only much farther on . . . something . . . happened . . .'

She, while she is talking, hopes, she realizes that she is hoping that she will meet the woman the one who told her about the novel, again. Somewhere, she is sure, at home she has a plastic bowl, a square one, which might be large enough for feet.

'Go on Miss Harper!' Dobby Borden says. 'Along this road, now tell us what happened.'